The sheriff—Tom Becker—knew Slocum well and liked him. Slocum slammed into his office and said harshly, "Tom, loan me your shotgun."

Becker took one look at the hard face with its flinty green eyes and nodded assent.

Slocum took the shotgun from the rack beside the door. Becker silently slid open a desk drawer and opened a box of shotgun shells. Slocum loaded the double-barreled gun, snapped it shut, and placed two more shells between the fingers of his left hand.

"Goin' after an army?"

"Mexico," Slocum said curtly without turning around.

Becker said, "Shit, not me. You're on your own, Slocum."

OTHER BOOKS BY JAKE LOGAN

RIDE, SLOCUM, RIDE
HANGING JUSTICE
SLOCUM AND THE WIDOW KATE
ACROSS THE RIO GRANDE
THE COMANCHE'S WOMAN
SLOCUM'S GOLD
BLOODY TRAIL TO TEXAS
NORTH TO DAKOTA
SLOCUM'S WOMAN
WHITE HELL
RIDE FOR REVENGE
OUTLAW BLOOD
MONTANA SHOWDOWN
SEE TEXAS AND DIE
IRON MUSTANG
SHOTGUNS FROM HELL
SLOCUM'S BLOOD
SLOCUM'S FIRE
SLOCUM'S REVENGE
SLOCUM'S HELL
SLOCUM'S GRAVE
DEAD MAN'S HAND
FIGHTING VENGEANCE
SLOCUM'S SLAUGHTER
ROUGHRIDER
SLOCUM'S RAGE
HELLFIRE
SLOCUM'S CODE
SLOCUM'S FLAG
SLOCUM'S RAID
SLOCUM'S RUN
BLAZING GUNS
SLOCUM'S GAMBLE
SLOCUM'S DEBT
SLOCUM AND THE MAD MAJOR
THE NECKTIE PARTY
THE CANYON BUNCH
SWAMP FOXES
LAW COMES TO COLD RAIN
SLOCUM'S DRIVE
JACKSON HOLE TROUBLE
SILVER CITY SHOOTOUT
SLOCUM AND THE LAW
APACHE SUNRISE
SLOCUM'S JUSTICE
NEBRASKA BURNOUT
SLOCUM AND THE CATTLE QUEEN
SLOCUM'S WOMEN
SLOCUM'S COMMAND
SLOCUM GETS EVEN
SLOCUM AND THE LOST DUTCHMAN MINE
HIGH COUNTRY HOLDUP
GUNS OF SOUTH PASS
SLOCUM AND THE HATCHET MEN
BANDIT GOLD
SOUTH OF THE BORDER
DALLAS MADAM
TEXAS SHOWDOWN
SLOCUM IN DEADWOOD
SLOCUM'S WINNING HAND
SLOCUM AND THE GUN RUNNERS
SLOCUM'S PRIDE
SLOCUM'S CRIME
THE NEVADA SWINDLE
SLOCUM'S GOOD DEED
SLOCUM'S STAMPEDE
GUNPLAY AT HOBBS' HOLE
THE JOURNEY OF DEATH
SLOCUM AND THE AVENGING GUN

JAKE LOGAN
SLOCUM RIDES ALONE

BERKLEY BOOKS, NEW YORK

SLOCUM RIDES ALONE

A Berkley Book/published by arrangement with
the author

PRINTING HISTORY
Berkley edition/August 1985

All rights reserved.
Copyright © 1985 by Jake Logan.
This book may not be reproduced in whole or in part,
by mimeograph or any other means, without permission.
For information address: The Berkley Publishing Group,
200 Madison Avenue, New York, NY 10016.

ISBN: 0-425-08031-5

A BERKLEY BOOK ® TM 757,375
Berkley Books are published by The Berkley Publishing Group,
200 Madison Avenue, New York, NY 10016.
The name "BERKLEY" and the stylized "B" with design are trademarks
belonging to Berkley Publishing Corporation.

PRINTED IN THE UNITED STATES OF AMERICA

FOR

Lewis Cummings: writer, weapons expert, soldier of fortune. He knew Mexico; fought with Villa; searched long ago for Maximilian's Treasure; and gave me his knowledge without stint. He, I hope, would have liked the cynical tone of this romance, set in that harsh and beautiful country.
*Amigo viejo,
mejor espejo.*

1

In the early autumn of 1884, John Slocum was working as an undercover range detective for the Cattlemen's Association of Arizona. Mexican rustlers, led by a man named Ismael Duran, had become much bolder over the last few years. Large herds were being driven across the border into Sonora, and any rancher who tried to stop them was immediately murdered.

Slocum was assigned to the area with Wesley Putnam. Putnam, who had come from Kansas, was ten years older than Slocum. The two men had taken a room in a hotel in Nogales, a town cut in half by the border. Slocum was sleeping on the bed with his sombrero tilted over his eyes to keep out the daylight.

Wesley walked into the room. He was five feet three inches tall and wiry as a rawhide reata. When he was angry, Slocum had seen Wesley's gray eyes take on the mean, unblinking stare of a diamondback poised to strike. Slocum had seen Wesley take on men six inches taller and put them down so fast they couldn't figure out what had happened to them. Wesley had been a Texas Ranger for six years and then quit after a fight with his captain. Wesley was in charge of this operation. Slocum liked him.

Wesley unbuckled his gunbelt and tossed it on the bureau top, thereby adding another scar to its already battered surface.

"Some day I'll get rid of this dang thing forever," he said. "An' I shore ain't gonna miss it."

"Guillermo was here," Slocum said, his eyes still closed. Guillermo Lopez was Wesley's informant. Guillermo worked as a porter and bartender in a cantina on the Mexican side of Nogales. The cantina was named *El Corazón de Sonora*. Slocum didn't trust Lopez, but if an experienced lawman like Wesley Putnam did, and was willing to pay good money to Guillermo, then the affair was Wesley's business and not Slocum's.

Slocum sat up, yawned, took off his sombrero, and carefully began to clean his Colt .44.

Wesley sank back in the battered armchair. "Yeah? Wha'd he say?"

"He said, *'El Pendejo a las siete.'*"

"The prick at seven," Wesley said with dour satisfaction. "It's a secret code. What time is it?"

Slocum could tell time within fifteen minutes whenever the sky was clear, day or night. "About a quarter to seven."

Putnam sighed, sat up, stretched, and stood up. He walked to the bureau and buckled on his gunbelt.

"Ol' *pendejo* be there at seven."

Slocum swung off the bed but Putnam lifted a hand. "I want a li'l talk with 'im. I'll go alone, so's he won't turn skittish. If he don' listen to reason, I'll bring 'im in."

"I—" Slocum began.

Putnam held up a hand. "You ain't me, John. I'll handle this my way. I allus have."

Slocum watched the little man walk out. He didn't like the whole setup. Meeting someone alone in Mexico was never healthy. But when Putnam said stay, he meant stay.

The cantina named *El Corazón de Sonora*—the Heart of Sonora—was a hundred yards south of the border. It was a grimy place, where the sole business of the patrons was to get drunk as quickly as possible on *pulque* or, if they had a little more money, on tequila.

There were scarred and *pulque*-sodden tables on both sides of the cantina. Down the center aisle thus created there was a single table which faced the entrance. Guillermo stood behind the bar, carefully washing glasses in a wooden bucket half filled with dirty, soapy water.

"*Cerveza*," Putnam said.

Guillermo paled and stared into the bucket. Putnam said softly in Spanish, so that only Guillermo could hear, "Where is the prick?"

A man sitting at the center table stood up and shouted, "*Aquí, gringo!*"

Since only Putnam and Guillermo knew the code

word, Putnam knew instantly that Guillermo had betrayed him. But before Putnam's hand reached his gun butt four men fired at him. All the bullets hit him. Putnam buckled and slid down to a sitting position. His left thigh had been broken by a heavy slug. Duran walked over and kicked the range detective's gun across the room. Putnam was mortally wounded. He stubbornly crawled into the street and headed painfully toward the border. Duran and the three others followed him along the dusty street, jeering and spitting at him. When he was a hundred feet from the border they kicked his ribs and then Duran fired a shot into the base of his spine.

The street emptied immediately. The paralyzed Putnam tried to drag himself on his elbows.

Slocum heard the distant shots from his hotel room. He raced downstairs and along the street until he reached the dying man.

"I'll get a doctor, Wesley!" he said.

"Hold on, John. No time. There were four. The leader seemed to be Ismael Duran. Two, a fellow, looked half-Mexican, half-Yaqui, mebbe. Three, a skinny feller with a pale face like a fish belly. How many's that?"

"Three. Wesley, hold on, you'll be all right—"

"John. Shut up. Fourth man, dark, had two teeth missin' in upper left jaw. Got that?"

"Got that. Wesley—"

"Repeat."

Slocum repeated, word for word.

Putnam almost smiled. "I c'n rely on you, John?"

Slocum stared at him.

"If you say yes, John, I c'n go peaceful," Putnam gasped.

Slocum's throat felt as if a great hand were squeezing it.

"Yes," he said.

The sheriff, Tom Becker, knew Slocum well and liked him. Slocum slammed into his office and said harshly, "Tom, lend me your shotgun."

Becker took one look at the hard face with its flinty green eyes and nodded assent.

Slocum took the shotgun from the rack beside the door. Becker silently slid open a desk drawer and opened a box of shotgun shells. Slocum loaded the double-barreled gun, snapped it shut, and placed two more shells between the fingers of his left hand.

"Goin' after an army?" Becker asked.

"Mexico," Slocum said curtly, without turning around.

Becker said, "Shit, not me. You're on your own, Slocum."

Slocum paid no attention. He hadn't expected any other response. He went out the door and into the dusty street. People recoiled nervously when they saw his face. He crossed the border, taking long strides. When he reached the cantina he knocked the swinging doors apart with the butt of the shotgun. Guillermo Lopez had just dipped a bundle of old rags into a bucket of water and was bending down, preparing to mop up Wesley Putnam's blood.

The *alguacil*—sheriff—was standing at the bar with his arms folded across his chest while he talked to Lopez. A few *vaqueros* were drinking *pulque* at one of the tables. Everyone became quiet and looked silently at Slocum. The *alguacil*'s hand drifted toward his gun butt. Without a second's hesitation, Slocum fired one shell at the mirror behind the bar. The blast in that confined space was so loud that the men winced. The *alguacil's* hand froze in mid-air. Slocum broke the gun, pulled out the used casing, dropped it on the floor, and reloaded so quickly that no one was able to move.

"*Todos afuera!* Everyone outside!"

Slocum stood with his back against the doorjamb, holding one side of the swinging door open. Cheesecloth hung in the door opening. It was used as a cheap fly-screen. The double barrels were pointed at the group. Both hammers were back.

Slocum ordered the men to rip the door off its hinges. They pulled it away, not daring to make any sudden moves. They walked down the street carrying the door, Slocum a few feet in back of them. When they reached Putnam's body no one said a word. They put his bloody corpse on the door and carried it into Arizona.

Slocum watched them turn around and return, without a word. Guillermo Lopez sighed in relief. Slocum noticed. Lopez had just made a mistake. He thought that this was the last he would see of Slocum.

Slocum had that most important quality of the best hunters: absolute patience.

He wanted each of the four murderers to be perfectly sure that Slocum, who had built up a reputation along the border for being merciless and unrelenting, was no longer a threat to them. He continued to work on the Circle W ranch, where he had been working together with Wesley. The owner, Howard McKenna, was a sour, bitter old man. Slocum had lost interest in finding out who among his fellow cowpunchers might be doing the rustling although, of course, he had some theories.

As far as McKenna was concerned, Slocum was just a saddle tramp drifting from ranch to ranch. He did his job competently and kept to himself quite a lot ever since his friend, Putnam, had been killed in some drunken brawl down in Nogales.

Slocum never told anyone the true story of that incident, nor did he report it to headquarters. It was his business to take care of, and no one else's. He wanted no advice from anyone. Once he rode up to Tucson and visited a print shop run by a man who could keep his mouth shut. The printer ran off just one copy of something that Slocum wanted for future use.

And Slocum waited.

And he drank. He drank a great deal. He started dropping into *El Corazón de Sonora*. He drank a great deal of the sour, milky *pulque*. He asked no questions. He knew very well that Guillermo Lopez watched him narrowly each time he came in. Slocum had built himself a reputation along the border towns as a bad man, usually very quiet, who could suddenly explode into violent action. Lopez kept his distance from the American. He hardly ever took his eyes from Slocum each time he came in to drink.

Slocum always got drunk. He mumbled how much he'd like to kill the bastards who'd shot Wesley. All he wanted to do was get hold of them. He'd cut their balls off, he told anyone near him.

But he did nothing.

Slowly the conviction came to Lopez that Slocum

had changed—that he was now nothing but a loud-mouthed braggart who couldn't handle his liquor.

So Lopez sent word to Ismael Duran that Wesley Putnam's old partner was no longer a man to be worried about. He sent the same information to the other three murderers.

And Slocum waited. He knew how to wait. Toward the end, he deliberately drank so much that he could not walk. He slid to the floor of the cantina and vomited. As he lay there, unable to move, he heard Lopez say, "*Cobarde!* Coward!" Then he felt a sharp kick in the ribs. Slocum lay inert. A bucket of dirty water was dumped on top of him. Still he did not move. Then Lopez grabbed him under his arms and dragged him roughly to the street. Lopez's parting gesture was to spit on him. Slocum still did not move. But Lopez would have felt terror had he seen Slocum's face. A slow smile had appeared on it. It was time to move.

2

One night two months after Putnam had been killed, Slocum rode across to Nogales and out past the *Corazón de Sonora*. The dirt road wandered in and out of the cactus. Two miles farther on he came to Lopez's little shack. It was surrounded by a hedge of cactus, which served to keep the goats out of his garden, where he grew tomatoes and chili peppers. A yellow light glowed through the small window. Slocum dismounted, dropped the reins, and moved silently to the window. Lopez was sitting cross-legged on a pile of dirty blankets in a corner. He was sewing a tear in an old pair of pants.

Slocum opened the door without any warning. Startled, Lopez, looked up.

Slocum said quietly, "We're gonna have a little talk, Guillermo." He sat down opposite the man.

"I don' know nothin'. We got nothin' to talk about, *hombre*. Get out."

He could not keep the contempt out of his voice. Although he himself was a traitor—had he not betrayed Putnam?—he despised a man like Slocum, who got drunk instead of avenging a dead friend. He thought Slocum was drunk, still on the long debauch he had begun the day after Putnam died.

Still sitting, Slocum half rose and kicked Lopez in the solar plexus with the pointed toe of his boot. Lopez fell to the dirt floor on his knees gasping for breath. He was temporarily paralyzed. He clutched his stomach with both hands; a look of astonishment swept across his face that this inert drunk could move with such speed, accuracy, and power.

"Guillermo."

Lopez said nothing. He was contorted in agony.

"*Guillermo*," Slocum said quietly. He bent down and grabbed Lopez by his hair and twisted his head so that he was forced to look upward into Slocum's face.

"What?"

"That's better," Slocum said. "Now listen carefully or I will hit you again. You told Wesley that Duran would come to the cantina at seven. And then you told Duran that Wesley would be there. So Duran and the three others showed up. Am I right so far?"

Lopez said nothing. Slocum banged his head sharply against the chair. Lopez moaned and then nodded.

"Good," Slocum said. "That means you're responsible for Wesley's death, Guillermo."

Lopez kept a throwing knife in a sheath tucked inside his belt. His loose shirt camouflaged the hilt. With both hands clutching his stomach, it was easy to pull the knife. As his arm went back for the throw, Slocum's Colt appeared in his right hand.

He fired. The bullet knocked the blade out of Lopez's hand, went through the wall of the shack, and screeched across the *mesquital*.

It became absolutely clear to Lopez that no drunk could draw so quickly and fire so accurately. It was also clear to him, with sickening conviction, that Slocum had been putting on an act all these months. Slocum pulled back the hammer and pointed the muzzle at Lopez's heart.

Guillermo Lopez held up both hands. "No, *no!*" he shouted. "What you want to know, *hombre?*"

Slocum let down the hammer. "The names of the three besides Duran. Where they live."

"What then?"

"Then you live, *hombre*. Then *you* live."

The three besides Ismael Duran were, first, Basilio Novarro, *mayordomo* of a horse-breeding ranch called the Five Wounds, in honor of the five wounds of Christ on the cross. The ranch was on the Rio Conchos. Then there was Hector Ruiz, who had fled to his mother's house in Guerrero; and, finally, there was Alejandro Robles, who lived in the Sierra near Tlaltenango, sixty miles north of Guadalajara.

Slocum extracted all the details and memorized them.

Lopez's hand was still tingling. He shook it while he clutched his aching stomach with the other.

"Listen good, Guillermo," Slocum said. "I could

make sure that none of those *cabrones* will ever hear of our talk if I kill you right now. But I'm going to let you live because of the help you gave me without too much trouble."

Lopez flushed at Slocum's contemptuous tone. He knew then who the coward was.

"If I ever find out," Slocum went on in a conversational tone, which somehow Lopez found more terrifying than if Slocum had yelled at him, "if I ever find out that you've gotten in touch with any of them— or told anyone about our talk—I'll kill you. *Comprende?*"

"*Sí,*" Lopez mumbled. The goddamn *gringo* had fooled him.

Next morning Slocum, without a word to anyone, quit his job and collected his back wages. He rode into Sonora at night, giving Nogales a wide berth. His saddle slicker was wrapped around a blanket; both were lashed to the cantle. In his saddlebags he carried a small can of salt mixed with a few grains of rice to absorb the moisture and prevent the salt from caking, a few strips of jerky for emergencies, a small frying pan and a metal cylinder full of friction matches, two pairs of socks, a spare shirt, and a bar of laundry soap. He wore a money belt containing thirty gold double eagles. Inside a piece of waterproof oiled silk he carried the piece of printing he had ordered specially made for him.

With that equipment he could ride across all Mexico in reasonable comfort. He rode a fine chestnut gelding named Joker. Slocum had bought it the year before from a broke gambler in Carson City.

Somewhere east of the Rio Bavispe, Lopez had

said, was where he would find Ismael Duran.

After two days of hard riding across the dusty, waterless chaparral of northern Sonora, Slocum came to the Rio Bavispe.

He crossed it and headed toward the Sierra. The ground tilted upward and soon became a perfect network of precipices and great mountains too steep to climb. It began to rain hard. A sheet of yellow water raced down the bare hillsides. It reached the valley and moved along it with a hoarse, sucking noise that made Slocum's horse nervous.

Somewhere in that range was Ismael Duran's camp. It was changed every few days, Lopez had said, in order to avoid ambush. It could be defended by one man with a rifle. Slocum climbed higher. Below, in a narrow canyon, the torrent of water twisted from side to side like a silver snake trying to climb the dark precipices that walled it in. The sky cleared and the roaring of flood water slowly subsided. Trees had been uprooted and swept in the cloudburst; they lay haphazardly along the banks of the river.

Slocum rode along slowly, looking for signs of Duran's camp. The chances were that he would not find it. His hope was that someone connected with Duran would accost him.

Slocum rode patiently. The air was clear and smelled of wet pine needles. The sun came out and the ground began to steam. His horse trotted around a bend in the narrow trail. A man levelled an old Springfield rifle at him. Two more stepped from inside a crack in the rock wall that lined the canyon wall. All of them wore old *huaraches*. They had the thin, pinched look of men who were constantly on the move. Their white cotton shirts and *calzones* were dirty.

"Manos arriba! Hands up!" The leader spoke in a bored monotone, as if he had been doing this all his life.

Slocum hesitated. If he yielded, and these were not Duran's men, they could kill him without any trouble. On the other hand, if he went into action and killed a couple—and they did turn out to be Duran's men— Duran would be furious and Slocum's plan to get close to him would be ruined.

He decided to go along. First, he removed his sombrero and bowed. *"Buenas tardes, Señores,"* he said pleasantly. He put his hands up. The men had probably never been so addressed in their entire lives, and they looked startled, then pleased. They broke out in grins.

"That's a very good horse," a tall, thin peon declared. "There has been rain ahead. He might fall and injure you. To prevent this calamity, it would be best for you to give him to me."

"Your logic is excellent," Slocum replied, still in the same pleasant tone. "However, I have promised to deliver this horse to Ismael Duran."

Their faces fell. Slocum let out a small sigh of relief. He had come across Duran's men, then. The leader of the group, Salvador Gomez, had thought that the horse of this stupid *gringo* would be his at the expense of only one Springfield cartridge. The others had mentally divided Slocum's guns and gear among themselves. They lowered their weapons with a disappointed look, as if they were children from whose mouths someone had snatched some delicious candy. Gomez pointed up the trail, and said curtly, "Well, then, keep going."

As he rode, Slocum turned around and looked at them. Gomez spat angrily and turned his back to Slocum, who grinned and turned around to face whatever might be waiting for him.

"I hear you want to sell me your horse," Duran said, He was lying on his back on a canvas cot he had looted from an American engineer at a copper mine near Cananea, farther north in Sonora. His hands were clasped behind his head. The cot had been set up under an oak tree. His men were scattered around the tree. Some were sleeping on worn blankets, others were heating tortillas on hot stones. A crude corral had been built against a vertical rock face and several scrawny horses were penned in it. Forage was scanty in the mountains.

"That is what I said," Slocum replied. He kept his face under control.

"Suppose I simply took it?"

"I would not like that," Slocum said gently.

Duran's face flushed. He was not used to being contradicted. His hands came from under his head and he sat up abruptly.

"You would rather sell it?" he asked with a slight smile. His bodyguard had stiffened and become more vigilant. It would be hard to kill him and escape.

"No, I don't want to sell it," Slocum said.

"Then why—" began an angry Duran.

"I could see they wanted to kill me and take my horse," Slocum said. "So I told them you wanted it."

"So they stopped to think it over?"

"*Claro.*"

Duran chuckled. Then he said abruptly, "What is a *gringo* doing alone in the Sierra?"

"Looking for work."

"I don't like jokes, *amigo.*"

"No joke. I had to get out of the States in a hurry. And I have to eat."

Duran's face hardened into skepticism.

"Or they would have killed me for my ammunition," Slocum said.

Duran smiled. There was no amusement in it. *"Porque no?"* he said. "They are poor, you are rich."

"Me? Rich?"

"By comparison, *señor*."

Slocum felt a kind of admiration for Duran's precise, grammatically correct speech. When the *conquistadores* first arrived in Mexico they were accompanied by Franciscan priests from upper-class families. It was they who had taught Spanish to the Indians. Slocum never ceased to be amazed at how frequently, in the loneliest and most desolate areas, he came across Indians and peons who spoke graceful Castilian.

Duran's men, like suspicious watchdogs, kept staring at Slocum.

Duran was quick to notice Slocum's wary glance.

"They never leave me," he said. "I am essential to their struggle, you see."

"Struggle?"

"Against Diaz."

Porfirio Diaz was the dictator of Mexico. He ruled with an iron hand.

Slocum nodded. A skinny mongrel slunk by, searching for garbage scraps.

"Pablito!"

"Sí!"

"Come here."

Pablito moved up silently on his *huaraches*.

Duran nodded at the man's belt, where a knife

rested in its sheath. Duran jerked his head at the dog.

"Pablito, if this *señor* were to threaten me—and if he were this dog—no offense, *señor*—what would you do?"

Pablito's hand moved so quickly that it was a blur. The knife came out, turned over once, and buried itself to the hilt in the dog's throat. The mongrel let out a choked howl, staggered a few steps, and fell. Its legs quivered a moment, then stopped.

Pablito bent over and recovered his knife. He casually wiped the blood from the blade on the dead dog's thin fur. Duran flicked his fingers at the man and he withdrew. Slocum counted six men who watched every one of his movements carefully.

Duran noticed his gaze. "Diaz wants to kill me," Duran said. "But even if he managed to smuggle a man into the camp—a man who said he wanted to join me—he would have to kill these six as well, either before or after he kills me. And Diaz is not a man who inspires self-sacrifice."

"So you are safe."

"Oh, very safe." Without a change of expression Duran said, in a soft voice, "Unless you are looking for the reward."

This was news to Slocum.

"What reward?" he asked with genuine astonishment.

"Diaz is offering five thousand pesos for me," Duran said.

"I should imagine you are worth far more."

This was just the right note to take. Duran smiled broadly at the flattery. Then he said, *"Gringos* don't come to Mexico, to the Sierra Madre, unless they have a very good reason."

"I have a reason, yes."

"And what is it?" Duran's face showed skepticism.

Slocum reached for his saddlebag. The man with the knife put his hand on the hilt and the other five members of the bodyguard moved closer.

"Perhaps," said Slocum, "it would be better if I were to let you examine the contents of my saddlebags."

"Not necessary, *amigo*," Duran said, inclining his head at his bodyguard. "Just move slowly. But, as a precaution, and purely as a formal matter, it would be somewhat courteous to let me have custody of your guns. For a while, that is."

"Of course," Slocum said. It was a risk that had to be taken. His immediate acquiescence, he noted, resulted in the relaxation of tension in everyone. He set his Colt and his Winchester beside Duran. The Mexican rose and rummaged through the saddlebags, searching for weapons.

"Well, then," he said, and sat down again.

Slocum pulled out the sheet of paper he had had printed in Tucson. It was in both English and Spanish. Above an old photograph of himself, the text read:

WANTED DEAD OR ALIVE

On September 14, the man whose picture is shown murdered two bank employees during an attempted robbery of the First National Bank of Tucson. He is six feet one inch tall. He has green eyes and black hair. He has a scar on his right shoulder and a knife scar on his lower back. He is to be considered extremely dangerous. He is an excellent shot. He has no known confederates. Anyone with information contact the federal marshal in Tucson, Arizona Territory.

Duran set the paper down. "Show me," he said.

Slocum took off his shirt. Duran looked at his shoulder and then at his lower back. "Machete?"

"Saber."

"Saber?"

"During our Civil War."

Duran sighed. "You are lucky," he said. "Our civil war is always going on, here and there."

Slocum suppressed a grin at hearing this bandit pretending he had any other motivation than loot for his battle against the Mexican government. Duran slowly folded the poster. He was thinking. It was clear that he had been impressed by it.

He shrugged. "What do you want from me?" he asked.

"Revenge."

This was a word which, as Slocum had discovered long ago, always struck a responsive chord in Mexicans. To avenge an insult was a serious business, and no Mexican took such things lightly.

"Revenge for what?" Duran asked.

"Betrayal."

"Ah. You were betrayed?"

"Someone I was working with. At the last moment he said he was sick. So I went in the bank without him. And then—"

Duran held up his hand. *"Entendido.* Understood. You plan to go back and have a little talk when things have quieted down up north?"

Slocum nodded. His plan had worked. Duran was

looking at him with approval. "And until then?" the bandit went on.

"I will not rely upon charity, *señor*. I will pay for myself."

"I would not dream of asking you for any money. But, out of curiosity, how much do you have?"

Out of curiosity, hell, Slocum thought. Duran would kill him like a mosquito for the double eagles in his money belt.

"Nothing."

Duran frowned. "Then how, *señor*, will you pay?"

The conversation was going exactly the way Slocum had planned it.

"Very simple. I will borrow three or four of your men. I will go to Arizona, and with their help I will bring back a fine collection of cattle. You will pay me fifty percent of what they bring—"

Duran held up a hand. "Why do I need you, *señor*? I can go and get the cattle myself."

"Yes. But your little raids have aroused the countryside. They are watching all the roads and cow trails. Your chances of getting away with it are very small."

"True."

"And you don't know all the little valleys where the cattle will be getting fat. Nor do you know where the best grazing will be found on the way down to Sonora. Or where the water is on the way. Or the secret cow trails."

"You know them?"

"Very well."

Cattle that had grazed well and had plenty of water to drink would trail easily and weigh more when sold.

Duran thought. He was thinking that the men he might send with Slocum would watch the *gringo* closely. Once in Arizona they would be eating off the country and not deplete the minimal supplies of the mountain hideout. What could he lose?

"Seventy-five percent for me," Duran said.

Slocum recognized the national talent for bargaining. If things went the way he had planned, he would never be around to collect his share anyway. Nevertheless, he bargained grimly for a larger share. Ten minutes later they finally settled for a seventy–thirty split.

3

Slocum meant what he had said. He was going to steal the cattle from Arizona.

He hadn't liked working for the Circle W. McKenna, the owner, was a gruff, unpleasant man, who begrudged decent food for his help. It had been assumed that cowboys on the ranch were working hand in hand with Duran. In the course of his undercover work, Slocum had investigated all the little valleys, box canyons, creeks, and wells in that harsh country lying on the western slopes of the Huachucas. McKenna's suspicions had proved to have no foundation, but Slocum had discovered all the trails whereby stolen cattle could be easily extracted from the Circle W.

As for his conscience, he had none in this particular matter. McKenna was rich, paid his help as little as possible, and told the cook to economize constantly. If stealing the cattle would bring Duran into his grip, Slocum would have stolen four times the amount he planned on rustling for Duran. It would be a pleasure to impoverish McKenna by even a small amount.

Duran's men stared impassively at Slocum. He squatted beside Duran's cot. In his right hand he held a sharpened stick. He had scuffed a smooth area in the dusty soil with his boot heel.

"Here's the border," he said. "Here's the San Pedro. We cross on the right bank. We go up the right bank for a few hours. Then we move eastwards a little. That will place us right up into the mountains."

"The Huachucas?" Duran spoke with annoyance.

"Yes."

"Why not go right up the east bank?"

"We might be seen. Then we'll be met by a posse on the way back. Up here in the Huachucas there's no one."

"What about Apaches?"

"Yes, we can always bump into a war party. Whether they fight or decide not to, one thing is sure—they will not tell the ranchers about us."

"So you will risk Apaches?"

"*Seguro*. What will they do to three or four well-armed men who are keeping their eyes open? No sensible Apache would consider attacking and losing one or two warriors."

"I *never* went through the Huachucas," Duran said, with an air of finality. "And I am not a coward."

"No doubt you are not. Yet you forbid us to test our courage?"

This was another perfect thing to say to a Mexican. The men within earshot had been listening with increasing interest. Slocum's last statement made several of them glance at Duran with a challenging stare.

Duran was annoyed. "My friend," he said, sitting up, "that is not the point."

"But it is."

Duran flushed. He was not used to being contradicted. He did not like it. "If you want to make a fool of yourself, *amigo mio,* that is your affair. But I am not going to risk any of my men on such foolishness."

More men had come up. They were absorbed with the debate. Slocum had noticed their fascinated interest and decided to play on it.

"*Amigos mios,*" he said, turning toward them, "who is afraid to ride with me through the Huachucas?"

He looked directly at a big man with a dark brown face and huge, rowelled spurs on badly run-down boots. He was standing with his thick arms folded across his chest. His name was Alberto Sotomayor.

"*No tengo miedo,*" the big man growled. "I am not afraid."

"Nor I," said another man.

When Slocum said, "You will come with me?" they nodded vigorously.

So it was settled. Slocum's handling of the matter had effectively removed the decision from Duran, who yielded grudgingly. Yet, as Slocum knew, the man had little to lose.

After all, using a skilled cattleman, who knew where he could pick up a good herd, who knew good, well-watered, well-grassed trails whereby he could take the cattle to Mexico—what was stupid about that? He risked two men—that was all he was willing to risk—

but there were plenty of others if something went wrong. The *gringo* was a hunted man in the States, so he would want to get out of Arizona as quickly as possible, and come back to Mexico, where he would be safe from prosecution, and where he would collect his share of the plunder.

Duran let a wolfish smile appear on his face. Slocum was not in sight. He beckoned Sotomayor close.

"On the way back," Duran ended his instructions. "The night before you get here."

Sotomayor nodded. He had never questioned any of Duran's orders, and he saw no reason to question this one. He was to kill Slocum as he lay asleep in his blanket.

Slocum led the way along the ridge top. This formed the spine of the Sierra Madre Occidental. The two Mexicans were tense, and turned constantly in their saddles. This was traditional Apache country. It was a perfect and easily defended fortress. To it the Apaches retreated after their raids on isolated ranches, wagon trains, and towns. It had plenty of deer and was well-watered.

The men jumped at every sound. During the first night's camp, on the heights above Imuris, they heard turkeys gobbling all around them. This was one of the ways Apaches communicated with each other. But Slocum knew they never attacked at night. They preferred to wait till dawn, when each warrior could see what he was doing. Slocum also knew that Apaches firmly believed that evil spirits roamed at night. He posted Sotomayor as the first guard. He knew that the nervous man would not dare fall asleep. As for Slocum, he fell asleep immediately, and so gained a reputation for cold-bloodedness with the two tense Mexicans. There was no attack.

Next day they crossed a short range of fanged, narrow peaks in the middle of a broad valley. The wind began to blow without stopping. Dust storms scooted across the valley floor. Sometimes the dust was so thick that the men were forced to pull their bandannas across their faces in order to breathe.

The men talked quietly between themselves. Slocum knew he would have to be triply vigilant: against Apaches, against Duran, and probably against Sotomayor. The consolation was that he would not have to be vigilant against all of them at once. That night they did not hear any turkeys gobbling. Slocum felt that their obvious careful alertness was obvious to the Apaches, as well as their panoply of guns.

On the afternoon of the second day they crossed into Arizona. Now they were in the Huachucas. Here the clashes between the Apaches and the Spaniards had been long-lasting and violent. When the Americans took the country after the Mexican War, the Apaches had at first welcomed the Americans with delight, since they knew that the victors had fought against their ancient enemies. But the Americans brought in more mines, more cattlemen, and more settlers than the Spaniards had ever dreamed of. Soon the war parties began to leave on their raids once more.

The men jumped at every strange sound. Slocum did not see any signs of the Apaches' presence; he did not smell any roasting mescal, one sure indication of an Apache camp. The deer they saw did not seem excessively wary. That meant they were not being hunted much. All good signs. On the other hand, a traveling war party could be observing them from the next ridge, and they would never know it.

Slocum began to relax a little. On the morning of the third day they came to the southern boundary of McKenna's ranch. From now on, as he immediately told the two Mexicans, they would have to exercise enormous care, lest they be seen by Circle W cowpunchers. They took a dim view of groups of riders ambling across their territory, especially since the recent series of cattle raids by Duran.

Slocum did not allow anyone to cross the skyline unless he first reconnoitered. A horse and rider profiled against the sky could be seen for vast distances in the clear air of that altitude. And that could attract the sort of interested attention which could have disastrous ends.

Approaching a ridge, Slocum halted. He held up a hand. The riders behind him stopped. He handed his horse's reins to Sotomayor, who took them grudgingly. Slocum walked at a crouch when he neared the crest. He aimed at an oak or piñon growing on the ridge or very close to it. Nearing it, he went flat, removed his sombrero, and crawled till he was camouflaged by the branches.

He repeated this procedure till he saw, at last, the grassy valley he remembered. This was the place where McKenna liked to pasture stock before he trailed them up to the railroad at Benson. They would get fat there, and an easy amble up to Benson would let them weigh just as much. Down the one-mile length of the valley Slocum counted sixty-eight head. In the middle of the valley's northern wall was the box canyon he had in mind. It was a natural corral where they could hold their cattle till they gathered the rest. And no McKenna man was in sight.

• • •

By noon next day they had rounded up a hundred and twenty-eight prime cattle, mostly two- and three-year-olds, the kind that commanded the highest price at any cattle market anywhere.

"*'Sta bien, 'sta bien,*" Sotomayor muttered.

Two days' hard driving put the cattle across the border into Sonora. They saw no one on the way.

Sotomayor said, "This *gringo* is smart. Plenty of water and grass this way and very easy going."

Gomez said, "He also uses mesquite wood to boil coffee. No smoke. This means no Apaches. He is smart. It is a shame to kill such a man."

"Duran said kill. We kill. *Claro?*"

Gomez said reluctantly, "*Claro.* But when the time comes, I will make the road easy to travel."

Sotomayor shrugged.

Policarpo Gomez was half Indian. He had the copper skin and straight black hair of his Tarahumare mother. Although he was nominally a Catholic, he performed many of the rituals of his mother's people. He always carried *hikori*, the Tarahumara word for peyote, with him. He treated the little dried buttons with great reverence. He called it *Tio,* Uncle. He believed that when he was searching for it where it grew, it sang beautifully so that he could find it.

So Policarpo decided to make the road easy for Slocum by giving *hikori* to the *gringo*. He had come to admire Slocum. On his last night, the *gringo* would find his last road clearly marked with visions. If God was willing, the visions would be powerful, and so God would welcome him joyfully.

Duran had not said a word to Policarpo about *hikori*. All he had said was "kill."

"Tomorrow night," Sotomayor told Policarpo.

The cattle were content with the water and the grass. They were accustomed to the routine of the trail. Sotomayor was sure that he and Policarpo could handle them easily the rest of the way.

High up on the rock-strewn ridge an Apache boy of fourteen named Dahwito watched the herd file by in twos and threes into the valley below.

The valley with its water was a good place to wait for thirsty deer coming down from their browsing for a drink. He set down his bow and quiver of arrows and watched for a while in astonishment. He had never before seen so many cattle together; the mountains were avoided by Mexican cattlemen. The three men with the cattle were well-armed.

Dahwito counted the cattle carefully. He itemized the revolvers and the Winchesters; he noted that the ammunition belts were full, and this meant that the three men could withstand a lengthy attack by Apache warriors.

Two of the men seemed careless. The tall man at the point was constantly looking in all directions as he rode: around, up to the crests of the ridges, then to the back trail, then back to the ridges once more. He was clearly an experienced frontiersman. The warriors would have to be very wary about approaching that one. The other two would probably not be very difficult. Although Dahwito was only fourteen, he was almost a full-fledged warrior; Apaches started training early.

The boy slid down from the slope to carry his

information back to his *rancheria*. But not before Slocum had seen him. All he caught sight of was a flash of something black, like a crow's wing sliding past a rock. But crows tended to caw angrily at anything they considered unusual. And a herd of cattle in this upland country could certainly be considered outside the ordinary.

And Slocum had not heard a crow caw for hours.

He held up his hand and turned his horse broadside to the moving cattle. The lead cow stopped. The others obediently stopped and began to graze. Sotomayor rode up.

"We'll camp here," Slocum said.

"Why here?" Now that they were almost at the camp where Duran was waiting, he decided it was time to question Slocum's decisions.

Slocum stared at him. Then he sighed and said, "Apache sign."

"Then why *stop?*" Sotomayor demanded. "Better to push on, then!"

"I took you to Arizona," Slocum said patiently. "I brought you back. We will spend the night here," Slocum said, and began to tick off the points with his fingers, "because, one, *amigo mio,* the grass is short enough here so that it wouldn't conceal Apaches moving toward us; two, the cattle will have water and grass; three, the resting place I had planned for the night would have put us on a slope with very little grass and no water, so they'd be restless and easily stampeded by Apaches; four, because it is my decision. *Entendido, amigo?*"

Sotomayor considered himself insulted by the harsh tone of the last phrase. He started to respond, flushed, and placed his hand on his knife hilt. He looked up and caught Slocum's gaze. It was like chips of green ice. Sotomayor removed his hand and thought with malicious pleasure that the *gringo* would be dead sometime that night. The *gringo* kept staring at him. When Sotomayor turned his horse, Slocum blocked his way.

"Sotomayor," he said, very quietly, "I asked if you had understood."

Sotomayor wanted to knife him immediately. But he was smart enough to know that he was dealing with a man of exceptional vigilance. Slocum, watching the man's eyes flit from his knife hilt to his face, knew what Sotomayor was thinking.

Sotomayor finally growled, *"Entendido."*

Slocum turned his horse aside and watched him ride away. Everything had been so easy up till now, he thought. It was only natural for his luck to change. He knew he would have to watch Sotomayor very carefully till they reached Duran's camp. So now he had Sotomayor to watch as well as the Apaches, who were no doubt watching their every move right this second.

4

Peyote has a very bitter taste and an unpleasant odor. Policarpo, whose duty it was to make coffee, pounded the coffee beans. When Slocum was scanning the hilltops, Policarpo deftly dropped in two peyote buttons and pounded them together with the beans.

The hallucinogenic juice saturated the coffee grains. Satisfied that he had extracted all the juice, he tossed the peyote husks away. He prepared two more heaps of ground coffee, one for Sotomayor and one for himself. He did all this so calmly that Slocum, totally preoccupied with watching for Apache sign, and listening at the same time for unusual night sounds which might signal Apache presence—the gobbling of turkeys, the shrill yelping of coyotes—did not notice what Policarpo was doing.

So Slocum ate his broiled calf ribs, spooned up the beans liberally seasoned with chile, and drank his coffee. He immediately sensed a bitter taste. At the time he thought that this was a result of the water that had flowed over an alkali bed.

"I'll take the first watch," he said. He stood up, scraped away the scraps, wiped the tin plate with a bunch of dried grass, and mounted his horse.

The man on watch rode slowly around the grazing and sleeping cattle. They were reassured by someone familiar. Whoever it might be kept singing—Slocum had taught this to the Mexicans, who had never before trailed a herd—so that a dozing cow would not be scared to death by the sudden appearance of a horse beside her without warning, leap to her feet, and start a stampede.

Sotomayor shrugged. He had avoided talking to Slocum as much as possible. Policarpo looked at Slocum with a strange, almost affectionate stare. It was only later that Slocum realized that it was the expression of someone saying goodbye. He had always gotten along with Slocum.

Slocum was tired from the long day's riding and the constant scrutiny in every direction. Then suddenly, without any warning, the fatigue floated away. He felt utterly relaxed; it was as if all the problems that had been filling his mind during the day had vanished, never to return.

The deep blue color of the darkening night sky intensified to the most beautiful turquoise he had ever seen. He wanted to tell the two Mexicans to stop whatever they were doing to share this beauty with him.

The sound of the wind blowing across the grass boomed like a huge cello. It was so lovely that he wanted to ride around the herd and point this out to the Mexicans.

It was the first sign that the peyote was taking effect. Slocum did not realize it.

"They will expect us to attack just after sunrise," Eskiminzin said. "So we will not. We will attack as soon as the evening star appears."

"Too dangerous," Juh said.

The eight Apaches were sitting cross-legged in a circle around Diskay, the war chief. Their faces were painted black for war. They were naked except for breechclouts. Their moccasins were pulled up knee-high because of cactus.

Each man carried a rifle gained in warfare against the Mexicans who lived on the lower slopes of the Sierra.

"Not dangerous," Eskiminzin said. "The tall man who was watching everything the past two days watches nothing any more. He looks at the sky, he stares at the grass. Something has happened to him. He is not looking at the cattle. So. We will come across the grass on the far side of the herd. Look!"

Slocum had dismounted. His horse's hooves had caught the fading light and their glossy surfaces seemed to him to have turned into four gigantic, flaring suns whose rays swelled into the most exquisitely beautiful reds and yellows he had ever seen. He held the reins in his hand as he knelt to examine the hooves. Then he laughed with sheer joy.

"Something is wrong with the white man," muttered Juh. "Maybe he is sick."

"Good," Eskiminzin said crisply. "We will go down right now. Through the herd, very low. When I bark like a coyote, three times, we kill. Is it understood?"

The war party nodded. Crouching, they crossed the ridge and filed down, slipping from one tree to another, using all the cover available. Slocum would have noticed them immediately if he had not taken the peyote. The two Mexicans had not seen the Apaches. Sotomayor wanted to come up behind Slocum and knife him in the kidneys to make his death as painful as possible. Gomez wanted to shoot him in the head so that he would die instantly, still enjoying his visions.

They were arguing the matter intensely but quietly as the Apaches reached the outskirts of the herd. The Apaches, as they moved among the cattle, kept up a steady, low humming noise. This soothed the herd. The Apaches began to edge toward the Mexicans and Slocum just as the next intense phase of his hallucination began.

Slocum sat back on his heels in astonishment. The four hooves had coalesced into a horsehair broom. The broom was on the landing of a staircase. Hundreds of doors opened onto the landing, which went on into infinity. The broom was being wielded by an unseen person. It was moving rhythmically, going inside and then outside one of the doors. It seemed perfectly natural that a broom might be held by invisible hands.

As the broom made its exit from each door the broom separated itself from the handle, and the strands moved across the landing like a procession of luminous caterpillars.

At the same time, an illuminated carpet slid out of the room. It had no end. It was the most beautiful greenish-yellow that Slocum had ever seen. It was so beautiful that it brought tears to his eyes.

Suddenly the broom vanished. The procession of the caterpillars ended. Slocum felt very sad, but in their place there began something just as beautiful.

The luminous carpet began to mount the stairs with a slow, serene ripple. Slocum sat cross-legged and stared at it in fascination. Then it suddenly turned into a long series of beautiful masks: animals, birds, snakes, people. He began to laugh in delighted amazement.

"Now," Sotomayor said.

Policarpo nodded. Now was the best time to kill Slocum. He would not even notice them as they approached. He would have no room for anything in his brain except the ecstatic visions he was seeing with such pleasure.

The two Mexicans stood up and walked toward Slocum. Slocum had curled up into the fetal position while he laughed at the marvelously colored, fantastic masks.

Sotomayor pulled out his knife.

"No," Policarpo said, putting a hand on his arm. "I will shoot him, as I said."

"Idiot! You will stampede the cattle!"

Policarpo had not considered that. While he was thinking over Sotomayor's remark, the coyote howled three times.

The men died quickly.

Slocum did not even know what had happened. He looked up and saw the black faces of the Apache warriors. He thought they were more masks from his visions and he smiled in appreciation of their beauty.

When Juh approached Slocum with his bloody lance, Eskiminzin held up his hand.

"He is either crazy or on a vision quest," he said sharply. "Leave him."

So the Apaches stripped the two Mexicans of their weapons and left Slocum, who kept laughing and chuckling as the night wore on.

Toward morning the hallucinations stopped. Slocum had been stretched out flat on his stomach. The sky was black. There was no moon. He was thirstier than he had ever been. On his way to the river, he stumbled over the bodies of Sotomayor and Policarpo.

His first reaction was that the two men had had a knife fight and killed each other.

But how was it that he had not heard a sound? He went to the river, drank his fill, and returned to the camp. The cattle were peaceful. Then he noticed, as the sky lightened quickly with the approaching sunrise, that his horse was grazing with its reins dangling on the ground. That meant he had dismounted and walked away from the horse. That had never happened before.

He wondered if he was going insane. Only when the light became stronger was he able to piece it all together.

First the moccasin tracks through the herd and around the two men. Then the huge number of lance wounds made by the Indians.

But their tracks were also around where he had

been himself. Clearly they had stood around him and just as clearly passed him by.

Why?

It was only when he noticed the pounded peyote buttons near the ashes of the cooking fire that everything fell into place: the bitter taste of the coffee, which he took for alkali water; the euphoria; the hallucinations. And that was why the war party had let him live. They must have thought he was a madman.

He had once chewed a peyote button at the invitation of a Yaqui medicine man. He had found the taste so bitter that he had only chewed it five or six times before he had spat it out. But it had been enough to give him some wild nightmares.

So either Policarpo or Sotomayor had put it in his coffee.

The question now remained: *Why?*

So he would not know what was happening around him? If so, *why?*

To kill him easily.

Again, *why?*

They would not dare to do such a thing without Duran's knowledge. So Duran had ordered his execution. And that made the second reason why Duran had to die. Once for Wesley, once for himself.

But softly, softly, was the way to catch a man like Duran. Slocum would have to bait the trap once more. And this time Duran wouldn't escape the jaws of the trap as they slammed shut on him.

Play dumb! Slocum told himself as he mounted. He found the lead cow and chivvied it toward Duran's camp. The herd obediently followed. They had been so well handled the past few days that he knew he could bring them in alone.

5

The sentries alerted Duran. He watched in amazement as the long line of cattle trickled into the valley, with only one man preceding them. The art of trailing cattle for long distances was a Texas invention of the 1870's, devised to bring Texas cattle up to the railroad in Kansas, or up to Colorado and Montana to stock the new ranches starting up there. Mexicans knew nothing about the techniques that had been created to make it possible. As a result, Duran was astonished.

When the last one ambled in he grunted. He walked down and counted them. He made it one hundred and twenty-two. The fact that his two men were nowhere in sight had not yet registered.

"I make it a hundred and twenty-two, *amigo*," Duran said, looking up as Slocum rode up wearily.

Slocum found it very hard to keep his face amiable, but he forced himself to smile in a friendly manner. "I beg to differ, *amigo*," he said. "One hundred and twenty-seven." That was another thing that cattlemen trained in Texas were able to do—look at a herd and count it very quickly. "We killed one for beef," Slocum went on. "None lost on the way."

Duran was impressed, and showed it. It still had not registered that his two men were not in sight. He was probably thinking that they were around somewhere. If he wondered why Slocum was still alive, he was waiting patiently for the answer, which would probably come from Sotomayor.

"Oh, very good, *amigo, very good!*" Then he added, "Where are those two lazy bastards? Screwing?" The camp had several women, who functioned as laundresses and part-time whores. None of them had appealed to Slocum.

"Dead."

"*Dead!* How?" Duran's face turned hard and wary.

"They were killed by Apaches last night."

It was clear that Duran didn't believe him, so Slocum said, "Ride back about fifteen miles. You will see everything that happened. As for me, I am tired. I must sleep."

He unsaddled and slapped his horse. It trotted off to join the others in the remuda. He unrolled his blanket and spread it in the shade of an oak. He fell asleep immediately, while Duran sent his best tracker, a Yaqui named Jaime, to check on Slocum's story. Six well-armed men rode with Jaime to protect him against the Apache attack which, Duran was sure, would never materialize. He believed that Slocum was lying.

Slocum was still asleep when the group returned late that afternoon and reported to Duran.

Duran said to Slocum, "Slocum, it happened as you said. They were not careful. But because of you I have lost two good men."

"Who did not do what they were supposed to do," Slocum said with a smile.

Duran was not sure of the implications behind that remark. His face showed no emotion.

Slocum went on, "But you have gained a hundred and twenty-seven fat *vacas,* which can either be sold at a fine profit or butchered from time to time to feed your men without the local ranchers becoming angry and putting pressure on Diaz to start another column on its way here to try to wipe you out. Their hides can be used to make reatas, make corrals, made *huaraches.* And you have also learned that I keep my word."

"That is true," Duran said slowly.

Slocum was sure that the man was seeing how he could accept this defeat and make a profitable conclusion out of the new situation.

"From the way you handle cattle, I believe you could have taken the herd and turned them back and sold them somewhere at a good profit," Duran observed.

"But first killing your two men?"

"First killing them, naturally."

"But I gave you my word that I would bring you the cattle."

Duran nodded thoughtfully. Slocum decided that Duran was thinking, yes, he had lost two men, but they were clearly incapable of carrying out their assigned task. On the other hand, he had acquired a very accomplished henchman, even though he might be a *gringo*. And he was a *gringo* with a well-motivated aversion to returning to the States permanently. A man who would have to live in Mexico. And that made a man with a certain reliability.

"Yes, you did," Duran said.

"And now I have another idea. A much better one."

"How many men will I lose this time?"

Slocum looked at Duran and said nothing. After a few seconds Duran remembered that Slocum had brought him the herd when he didn't have to, and that the men had been killed because of their own carelessness.

Duran was incapable of apologizing, but he did his best to soften his remark.

"Let me hear," he said.

"We will go much further this time into Apachería," Slocum began, but Duran angrily interrupted.

"How can you guarantee that the men will survive? It is nonsense! The Apaches have done well, killing my two men, taking their guns, and they will certainly try again! And with many more warriors, there is no doubt about that!"

Slocum waited patiently until Duran had finished. "We will not take the cattle through Apache country."

"It is just as risky in the flat country, with all those *gringo* ranches forming their posses! No, to do another raid now would be stupid."

The bodyguard nodded in agreement. Duran, Slocum noticed, had already added two men to it to make up for Sotomayor and Policarpo. They were six again. They had the hard, unblinking stares of eagles. Their heads turned to watch every move of Slocum's. Their hands were always close to their gun butts or machetes.

"Yes, it would," Slocum said calmly. "But we won't be going that way."

Duran quieted immediately. He lifted a hand, palm up, and swept it sideways. It was an invitation to proceed.

"Do you know the Plains of San Agustin?" Slocum began.

Duran shook his head.

Slocum went on, "It's a broad, very well-grassed, well-watered valley about twenty, thirty miles long, two miles wide, west of the Black Mountains. They are west of Socorro."

"Yes. I have heard of this town. It is on the Rio Grande, not far from Albuquerque."

"Correct. Fat cattle are all over the Plains. Sixty miles north is the railroad. Three days' hard driving. Some desert, but there are wells and creeks. I can put the cattle straight into cattle cars on the third night. There is a corral at a siding. No questions asked." He rubbed his thumb and forefinger together.

Duran's eyes widened. "Then?"

"We take the cattle and push them north."

"How many, do you think?"

"A thousand, eleven hundred."

"What!"

Slocum said easily, "The grass is so rich and there's so much of it that they graze next to one another. No spreading out, one cow to a hundred acres, like they do down in Sonora." Slocum had decided to go all the way with his fairy tale as soon as he saw how greedily Duran was drinking in his fantasies. The credit he had built up by bringing the hundred and twenty-seven head back from McKenna's place with such expertise was working for him. But it would not do to make it all sound too easy. A line had to be drawn.

"But I'll need seven, eight men."

Duran became thoughtful. "Seven? So many men traveling all that distance will attract much attention, *amigo*."

"Not if they go the way I've chosen."

"What's that?"

"Cross the border east of the Huachucas. Up through the Dragoon Mountains."

Duran interrupted. "But that's Cochise's hideout!"

"Yes. But he'll never attack seven well-armed men. And, since every one else avoids that range, no one outside of Apaches will see us."

"Then?"

"Then we cross the Gila—at night—just in case someone might be watching. We go into the San Franciscos and ride a couple hundred miles north, all through mountain country, plenty of deer and good water. Again, since it's Apache country, we won't meet anyone. Then we move east and come out where the Plains of San Agustin begin. We drive the cattle before us till we have what we want. Drive them north to the railroad."

"But it's mostly Apache country," Duran repeated.

"Seven well-armed men—and me—keeping a sharp watch? They'll be safe. I will see to that."

"So it's all the way through Apache country?"

Slocum looked at Duran. He said patiently, "It's the only way not to be noticed."

"But—" Duran began.

Slocum lifted a hand. "Who would expect the terrible Duran to raid so far away from his usual places?"

Duran began to smile. Slocum had hit the right note: an exploit which could be commemorated in the *corridos*, the ballads which would be written and sung about Duran afterward.

"This McKenna—he must be going crazy trying to find his cattle, hey?"

"Yes. And every rancher along the San Pedro is staying up nights waiting for your next raid."

"But we'll go far to the northeast instead? Never have Mexicans raided so far into your country!"

"You will make history."

"Por Dios!" Duran almost shouted. "And I will go with you!"

"Excellent."

"You can show me the trails!"

And be in at the payoff too, you suspicious bastard, Slocum thought. Slocum almost felt indignant until he realized that this expedition would never take place. It was clear that Duran did not fully trust him with handling the cash he would get from the imaginary sale of the nonexistent cattle. It was pretty funny, when Slocum thought about it.

Duran was thinking that the *gringo* did not want to be in the States in case he got caught and hanged, but what would prevent him from taking the money and disappearing into Canada?

He put that thought aside. The solution was simple—go along with Slocum and handle the money himself. He laughed with joy. "Now, you will be my guest," he said happily. "Tonight we will ride to Magdalena and drink good tequila and get us some women in the best whorehouse in Sonora. And afterwards we will discuss the details of this marvelous plan. I will show you I know how to reward good men. Baltasar!

Gregorio! Jesus! Saddle up, we are going to Magdalena!" He turned to Slocum. "They have a new Chinese girl. She knows such things you would not believe. She will be yours. I give her to you!"

So the bodyguard would consist of only three men this time. Four, with Duran. Bad odds, but somewhat better than before. Duran was beginning to trust him. Slocum reined his impatience.

Be very careful, he told himself. *Choose the time carefully. You will not have a second chance.*

The ride to Magdalena took four hours. They arrived after dark. Mongrels snapped and barked as they neared the outskirts of the town. Duran was in high spirits. He deliberately spurred his horse at a dog that had planted itself in the middle of the road. The dog was too slow getting out of the way. Slocum heard the dog's spine crack. Duran laughed and looked over his shoulder at Slocum for approval. Slocum smiled back. He was thinking that this would be the final performance that the son of a bitch would be getting from him.

"This is the best place in Sonora," Duran boasted as he leaned forward in his saddle and seized the old iron knocker. "You will see!"

The knocker, shaped like a rearing dragon, had come from China via the Manila galleons long ago. Duran slammed it against the massive oak door. Bougainvillea vines grew over the door in a profuse avalanche of red bloom. An Indian maid opened the door.

Slocum caught a glimpse of cool white tile floors and a big clay olla crammed full of purple jacaranda. Two kerosene lamps hung from a ceiling beam.

"Pasen, señores," the maid said.

Duran dismounted and tossed the reins to Baltasar, the biggest of the bodyguard. Slocum dismounted. Baltasar took the reins of his chestnut as well and, with the other men, tied them at the hitching rack. Slocum noted carefully that the rack was on the east side of the building.

The rest of the bodyguard, hands on gun butts, followed Duran and Slocum into the house. Duran said, "Oh, Diaz would like to get me, but he won't, not with my men." The bodyguards took up their stations as soon as they walked into the big room: one at each door, one at each window, and two at the foot of the staircase.

Duran wanted full protection but he drew the line at having people in the room while he was screwing. Nor did he want any within earshot. Slocum puzzled about that for a while as Duran led the way upstairs. It would be a perfect time to shoot him in the back, the way he had helped assassinate Wesley, but his men were watching carefully from the foot of the stairs.

Later. He would kill him later. It had better be soon, because he did not know if he could rein in his fury any longer every time he thought of the bullet-riddled, fractured body of Wesley.

As they climbed the stone staircase, the smell of perfume grew stronger. Duran opened a door. A long couch covered with yellow silk was against the far wall. Four women lounged along its length. One was a blonde who wore a red dress cut low enough to expose her breasts down to their nipples; two were black-haired *mestizas,* pretty enough, who wore simple white cotton dresses such as their mothers might wear; and the fourth girl was Chinese. She wore a black silk dress with a dragon motif in red writhing around the dress in a long spiral.

The blonde was running her hand up inside the slit skirt of the Chinese girl. The two *mestizas* watched with dignified reserve.

Duran said, "The blonde is French! Think of that, *una Francesa!* The Chinese girl comes from Manila. She knows such things! No one in Mexico knows what she knows, believe me. And, since we are partners, you shall have her."

He snapped his fingers at her. The blonde took her hand away and looked at Duran with a mixture of annoyance and fear. The Chinese girl got up sinuously. Without a word she came to Duran, took his hand, and rubbed it against her groin.

"She is very hot," observed Duran. "The French girl! Did you see what she was doing? I will take the French girl. Later we shall compare our experiences. How do you like the idea?"

"Excellent."

Duran took the French girl, who went with him reluctantly. They disappeared into the room to the left of the parlor. The Chinese girl led Slocum into the room beside Duran's. Two of the bodyguards watched Duran with big grins as he closed the door to his room. Then they sat back in their chairs to watch the staircase.

Slocum's room contained a big bed with clean white cotton sheets, a feather pillow which smelled clean, and a big wardrobe in a corner next to a window. On a low dresser near the wardrobe stood a white enamelled wash basin, a pitcher of water, two neatly folded towels, and a bar of soap on a small marble soap dish.

As Duran had said, it had elegance.

But most important for Slocum was the window. Slocum pushed open the two tall wooden shutters that covered it. Mexicans believed that night air caused all sorts of diseases. The girl watched him with grave interest. There was a drop of thirty feet to the ground. He closed the shutters and turned around. The Chinese girl had pulled off her dress and was hanging it in the wardrobe. She was naked underneath. She had a long waist and her long black hair, shining and sleek as a seal's, fell in a smooth, unbroken fall down her pale almond-colored skin to her small, firm buttocks. In profile were her hard little breasts. They jutted sharply. On their upward tilt, at the apex, there perched two perfect little red cherries.

Slocum next walked to the bed. He picked up the nearest edge of the bedsheet and tried to tear it. It resisted. When he exerted much pressure it ripped. Good. It was strong enough to hold his weight when he would be going down from the window.

The girl was staring at him in silent puzzlement. She walked close to him, unbuckled his gunbelt, coiled it neatly, and set it down on the marble top of the dresser. She knelt in front of him and pulled off his boots. She stood up and undressed him, letting her fingers linger on his genitals, and hung up his clothes neatly in the wardrobe. She beckoned him closer to the dresser. She poured warm water into the basin from the pitcher, soaped him, and washed him thoroughly. She dried him off with the thick towel, gently patting his testicles and penis. They swelled under her deft touches.

She pulled him to the bed. From the next room, where Duran had gone with his French blonde, there came a muffled cry of pain. The Chinese girl seemed slightly worried, but not too anxious, as if this was a normal occurrence when Duran showed up.

Slocum lay on his back. She knelt on the floor and began to kiss his legs, darting her hot, wet tongue in and out. Slowly she moved her lips upward, while her fingertips reached even higher and gently stroked his scrotum. When his penis became rock-hard, she reached out with both her hands and stroked its entire vein-engorged length. Somewhere, without Slocum having noticed it, she had rubbed a fragrant oil onto her palms.

The sensation was exquisite. A whimper escaped from Duran's room. But Slocum put that aside from his consciousness; he wanted to savor the supremely skillful handling by his girl.

He reached up and cupped her sharp little breasts in his hands. The hardened nipples dug into his palms. She shuddered as the calloused skin scraped them. Then she gasped with pleasure and went on with her stroking. Slocum wanted to push her on her back and screw her; she sensed this, and pushed his shoulders back. "Later," she whispered into his ear, and stuck her tongue into it.

Her arms went under his back and turned him over onto his stomach. She put him into a kneeling position. Then she left him for a moment. He turned to see what she was doing. A muffled grunt and a sob of pain came from the room next door. What was the son of a bitch doing?

The Chinese girl opened a drawer of the dresser. She took out a twenty-inch length of string. She efficiently tied a knot in it every two inches along its entire length. When she had made eight expertly spaced overhand knots, she suddenly pulled the string hard at both ends. Each knot became hard as a rock. Satisfied, she turned, smiled at Slocum's puzzled face, and rubbed her palms with the same fragrant oil. Now Slocum recognized the scent. It was sandalwood.

She opened the door and called out, "Luisita!"

One of the *mestizas* appeared. She smiled shyly at Slocum while the door was closed behind her. She pulled off her white dress. She was full-breasted. She spread herself flat on her brown stomach on the bed in front of Slocum, reached up with her hands, and began stroking his penis. The Chinese girl knelt behind Slocum and caressed the length of his hardened penis with one oiled palm while with the other hand she delicately stroked his scrotum. The sensation of the four hands stroking his cock and balls was almost too much for Slocum. He held back with difficulty. When the Chinese girl sensed he was about to ejaculate she held back; thus Slocum could control himself.

Suddenly he realized what she was doing with the string: she was inserting the knots into his rectum with her tongue, one by one. While she did that the *mestiza* started to slide her mouth up and down the outside of his penis; when his veins were massively engorged she put her mouth around the head of his penis, and began to slowly slide her wet mouth up and down, up and down, flicking with her tongue as she did so.

The Chinese girl continued to insert the string. It was not in the least painful; she had lubricated the string well with her saliva, and the rectal muscles had relaxed a little. When she had finished, the knots formed a small mass on top of the incredibly sensitive prostate gland.

54   JAKE LOGAN

When Slocum finally felt as if he could not hold back one second longer, the Chinese girl sensed that the proper moment had come. She touched the *mestiza's* mouth; the girl suddenly increased the speed of her lubricated suction, while the Chinese girl jerked the string out with a violent sideways jerk of her head.

As each knot rode over the prostate gland it gave the gland the lightest flicking stimulation, eight in a row. The hard knots multiplied the ecstasy unbearably. Slocum ejaculated harder than he had ever done in his life into the *mestiza's* mouth. She swallowed his sperm greedily. Then he fell flat, exhausted.

The Chinese girl rose. With a damp, soapy towel, she washed his genitals thoroughly. The *mestiza* smiled at him, rose, put on her dress, and then the three of them heard the muffled sobs from Duran's room.

"*Mucho malo*," the *mestiza* said with a frown. She went out of the room. Before the door closed Slocum could hear the bodyguard calling up to her. "*Ven acá, guapita!*" Baltasar shouted. "Come here, little rabbit!"

"*Si, yo vengo, yo vengo!*" she called downstairs. The door closed behind her. The Chinese girl made fists and pantomimed punching herself in her sharp breasts. Then she pretended to pinch her nipples violently. "*Malo*," she said, shaking her head. "*Malo hombre.*"

"*No más*, no more," Slocum said, gaining strength. She did not understand the implication and paid no attention.

"Oh, *si, más, más!*" she said, shuddering. Then she added, in her broken Spanish, "No can fuck, like to hit, maybe then. But not. Drink too much."

Sure enough, as if on cue, Slocum heard the sound of a fist striking flesh, followed by a pained whimper.

He started to get up, but she had oiled her palms again. Much to his surprise, her skillful work brought him quickly to an erection. Then she bent her head down and took him deeply into her throat.

Slocum dressed and buckled on his gunbelt. Since Duran had paid for her, there was no need to give her anything, but he dug out one of his gold double eagles and handed it to the girl. Her eyes widened. *"Para tú misma,* for yourself," he said. He put a finger to his lips, pulled the strong cotton sheet from the bed, and tore it into strips to make a rope. Her mouth opened in astonishment, but Slocum pointed to the gold coin she was still holding in her palm. She understood and subsided.

He tied one end to one of the massive mahogany legs of the bed. He coiled the rope and placed it next to the window. He placed a finger across his lips, picked up the big feather pillow, opened the door, and walked quietly to Duran's room. The bodyguards were talking animatedly to the two *mestizas* and did not see Slocum.

He opened the door. Duran was methodically beating the blonde whore. She was crouched on the floor in the corner of the room, covering her bruised breasts with her crossed arms.

Duran turned. There was an almost empty bottle of tequila on the dresser. Duran swayed, but kept his balance by placing one palm against the wall.

"Olá, hombre!" Duran called out when he saw the pillow. "You are not going to get into bed with this

puta. So get out! *Pronto!"*

Slocum moved closer. He had been waiting for this moment for months.

"I mean it!" Duran said, louder. *"Afuera! Ahorita!* Out! Right now!"

His friendly but irritated tone was quickly disappearing. When he saw Slocum's face, he realized finally that something was going to happen. Duran half turned and reached a hand to his gun, which was on the dresser.

"To die drunk," Slocum said quietly, "you lucky man." He pulled Duran around by his shoulder so that they were facing each other. "Wesley Putnam, you fucking bastard," he said, placed the pillow against Duran's chest, shoved the muzzle of his Colt deep inside the mass of goosedown, and pulled the trigger three times. The deeply stuffed pillow muffled the shots.

The whore opened her mouth to scream, but Slocum pointed the gun at her and placed his finger across his lips. She closed her mouth immediately.

The three slugs had torn Duran's heart to rags. He sank to his knees, shaking his head in amazement. He was still alive. His face convulsed and he started to say something. Slocum put his palm across Duran's mouth and shoved as hard as he could. Duran's skull clicked against the wall. The whore was sobbing quietly. She looked like she wouldn't be doing any yelling. Slocum moved into the hall and closed the door quietly. From the angle where he was, he could see the heads of Duran's bodyguards. One of them had a *mestiza* on his lap. She had buckled on someone's gunbelt, put on a wide-brimmed sombrero such as was worn in Chihuahua and Sonora, and crossed her arms. She was imitating Duran's typical frowning look. Based on the delighted chuckles of her audience, she was doing a good job. One of the bodyguards, more conscientious than the others, took a quick glance up and saw Slocum.

Slocum cursed, but he kept his face amiable, and waved in a friendly manner. The man smiled back.

Slocum walked into the Chinese girl's room. She had not moved. He dropped his rope outside the window. When he passed close to her she smelled the recently fired gun. She looked scared.

"Mi amiga? My friend?" she asked.

"All right."

"And the other one?"

"Dead."

Slocum put one leg outside the window.

A delighted smile spread across her face.

Below, Slocum quietly led away his horse. A hundred yards away, he swung into the saddle and rode for his life.

6

Slocum rode hard for the border. Early the next morning he crossed it a few miles east of Nogales. He rode west of the Whetstones, bore to the northeast, and rode along the length of Cienaga Wash till he reached the railroad. A few miles east brought him to Benson. He had three gold eagles left, not enough to finance extensive travels through Mexico.

So he sold his fine chestnut for five hundred dollars. For the saddle and Winchester he picked up another hundred and seventy-five.

He bought a ticket on the Texas Pacific and went east. He rode across the rest of Arizona, crossed New Mexico, and went on into Texas. He made his way down to Brownsville via local trains and stagecoach. He was fourteen hundred miles from Nogales.

At Brownsville he bought a suit of dignified black broadcloth and plain black boots. A gold watch and watch chain improved his disguise, since he planned to introduce himself as a buyer of fine quality horses. His narrow-brimmed Stetson completed his outfit. He bought—at a pawnshop, for the sake of its battered but expensive appearance—a good leather carryall. Into this he placed his spare clothing, his Colt and gunbelt, and a box of spare ammunition.

At Matamoros, on the Mexican side of the Rio Grande, he bought a ticket to Monterrey. The dilapidated *Ferrocarriles de México* train rattled and banged across the flat, dusty, chaparral-packed desert. The windows were either broken or covered with a thick layer of dirt that had only been washed by an occasional rain. Many were jammed into an open position. Once a sudden hard downpour blew rain into the car so heavily that everyone stood up on the far side till the shower ended.

At Monterrey he took a stagecoach for the eighty-five- mile run southeast to Linares. The horse-breeding ranch of the *Hacienda de las Cinco Heridas* lay thirty miles east, on the Rio Conchos.

The Hacienda was the most successful ranch of its kind in Mexico. Flinty outcrops over its four hundred thousand acres made for strong hooves, the grass was excellent for young colts because of the limestone soil, and the extensive divisions into big pastures secured by barbed wire made casual, indiscriminate breeding an impossibility. There were no wild horses to complicate matters.

The Hacienda was owned by a wealthy man named

Arturo Ramirez. His conquistador forebear from Extramadura, in Spain, was a cousin of Hernán Cortes, and was Cortes's right-hand man during the Conquest. As a reward he had been given this enormous ranch and its Indians. Generation after generation the Ramirez family and the Indians had worked on it and improved it. The first Ramirez had been cruel but devout, hence the choice of the name: The Hacienda of the Five Wounds—the five wounds suffered by Christ.

The current owner hated the provincialism of Mexico. He preferred to live on his large income in either Madrid or Paris.

His wife, Caterina, was a handsome, full-figured woman in her late thirties. She had a great sexual appetite which, since her husband was usually in Europe, was satisfied by her *mayordomo*, Basilio Novarro.

And Novarro was the second one on Slocum's list. Why the *mayordomo* of such a famous ranch should be in the sleazy border town of Nogales had been puzzling Slocum. But he found out the reason in Linares, while he was concluding negotiations with Alfredo Torres, who owned a large livery stable.

Slocum had bargained Torres down expertly from the fifty pesos a day he had demanded to rent one of his fine buggies with a decent horse. Torres was impressed with the way this apparently naïve *gringo* had unerringly picked out the best horse, and then idly, with amusement, how he had pointed out the various tricks Torres had been using to make some decrepit nags look younger.

Afterwards he won Torres's affection by leaving a healthy deposit.

Torres told him how to reach the Hacienda. He was bursting with curiosity about Slocum. Slocum casually mentioned that he had been traveling all over the southwest of the United States searching for a pair of matched bays, not older than three years old. A millionaire backer of President-elect Grover Cleveland wanted to present them as a surprise for the inauguration ceremony next March. He had had no luck until a horse dealer in San Antonio had told him to try the Hacienda of the Five Wounds.

"Oh, yes," Torres said, with a respectful tone. "No doubt you will find them. Novarro travels everywhere to find the best studs."

"Everywhere?" Slocum asked skeptically.

"Yes, everywhere! He travels to Texas, to New Mexico!"

"With your permission, that is not very far."

"He goes farther! He went as far as Arizona last time!"

Slocum looked impressed. "Did he find any good stock?" he asked.

"He *always* finds good stock. *Señor,* you will not find any place to eat between Linares and the Hacienda. I would be honored if you would lunch with me."

Slocum yielded. During the lengthy and delicious meal, Slocum picked up all the local gossip about Novarro and Caterina Ramirez.

"Old wives' tales," Slocum said as he spooned up the rich *flan*.

"Oh, no, it is all true. Everyone here knows it. The servants see and hear everything. They are Indians, they do not count, although they have souls worth saving, but they are not really there, you understand, not for people such as Caterina Ramirez, who is of the nobility of Spain. And if Ramirez himself does not care what goes on in his absence, why should anyone else?"

"Indeed, why?" Slocum agreed. He wondered how long it would take to discover the lay of the land. Not too long, he hoped. His money would be running out soon, and there would be two more after Novarro to take care of.

Toward eight that evening his buggy turned in at the road that led to the Ramirez hacienda. Slocum could see the massive house from miles away. It had been solidly built over two hundred and fifty years before by Indian labor. It was deliberately designed to resist a siege.

As Slocum approached the huge iron gates that barred access into the lavishly planted patio, peons working in the corn straightened up and leaned on their hoes to look at him. Strangers were rare at the hacienda. The corn was tall and full of almost ripe ears. Water was not a problem here, and Slocum could see, from the massive leaf canopy towering over the hacienda walls, that the vegetation inside was lush. In the pastures stretching back of the hacienda and going toward the distant blue mountains, Slocum saw groups of horses grazing here and there on the rich, abundant grass. They looked to be in superb condition.

A big man with an arrogant face passed out through the iron gate. A peon respectfully closed the gate after him. The man was riding a fine black stallion with indolent ease; he was a master horseman, Slocum could see. As soon as the stallion passed through the gate he pranced in sheer exuberance. The horseman, who had a neatly trimmed black mustache and wore charro trousers with a row of silver buttons down each side, controlled the horse expertly. He wore a wide-brimmed sombrero with a cord attached to it to prevent it from being blown off by sudden wind gusts.

The man saw the Indians staring at Slocum instead of working. He spurred the horse into a quick spurt into the corn field. He had a harsh, arrogant voice that matched his face. The men went back to their hoeing. Even their backs showed resentment at the insulting remarks. Satisfied, the horseman moved toward Slocum's buggy.

As the rider neared, Slocum removed his hat and bowed slightly. *"Buenas tardes, señor,"* he said, politely.

The man reined in. His eyes swept over Slocum and examined his clothes, then critically observed his horse and buggy. Like most servants of the rich and noble, he had calculated exactly how much deference everyone should receive. He kept his hat on.

"Qué quieres? What do you want?"

The abrupt statement was in very poor taste. So was his refusal to remove his hat, and finally, to Slocum's annoyance, was his use of the familiar form *"tú"*, instead of the more formal *"Qué quiere usted."* The man's choice showed that he considered Slocum an inferior.

"To business, then," Slocum said coolly. He replaced his sombrero. "I am an American," he began.

"A poor recommendation."

Slocum told himself that he must not lose his temper. "That may or may not be," he responded calmly. "I have come all the way from Ohio—"

"From *where?*"

"Ohio. One of the United States."

"A ridiculous name. I have never heard of it."

"Indeed?" Slocum said. His amused tone implied that the Mexican was living in a cultural backwater. "No matter. I have come here because I have heard that you breed the best horses in Mexico."

"That is so! And better than any in Ohio."

"Of course," Slocum said in an agreeable tone. "And that is why I have come here."

"Ah?"

"I am looking for a pair of flawless matched bays. They must be three years old, not younger, not older."

"For yourself?" The tone was scornful as the man looked at the inexpensive buggy.

"No. They will pull the carriage of the President of the United States at the coming inauguration."

The man's eyes widened as he calculated what he might ask for such a pair of horses. And the pleasure he would get recounting the story to friends—that the Americans could not find good horses in their own country, but were forced to come to Mexico for them.

"And you could not find them in Ohio, hey?"

"No. I have not been able to find a matched pair in Kentucky, nor in Texas."

"Texas!" the man said scornfully. By now Slocum was sure that this was Basilio Novarro, the *mayordomo*. "Skinny cow ponies, mustangs—what do they know of Arabian stock? Nothing! So you have traveled all over your States? And have given up? And have come to Mexico to buy horses for your *president?*"

Slocum nodded. Let the man feel good about it.

Novarro laughed spitefully. Then he considered that there could be a lot of money here if he controlled his contempt. The Hacienda would provide the horses, and a decent amount would stick to the *mayordomo's* fingers, most likely as a bribe.

"Yes," he finally said. "I can supply them. My name is Basilio Novarro. Welcome to the Hacienda de las Cinco Heridas. Drive up to the gate and say you are my guest. We will talk about this later."

Without waiting for Slocum to introduce himself, without a word of farewell—both violations of Mexican good manners—he trotted off abruptly.

He did not have a bodyguard. It would be quite easy to kill him. But first an escape route had to be plotted. The man was important, and the telegraph now covered most of Mexico. The murder of a Mexican citizen by an American would be treated very seriously. It would take careful planning.

Slocum saw Caterina Ramirez at dinner. She came down the wide staircase wearing a simple white cotton dress with a square neckline, the kind of dress one of her Indian maids might wear on market day. A thick strand of brilliant green wool kept her blonde hair in one thick honey-colored rope down her neck. She had green eyes, like Slocum. Her skin was pale and there was a dusting of freckles across her bare shoulders. She had a full bust and long, slender legs. Although her bust was full, it was well-proportioned to her height, which Slocum judged to be about five feet ten inches without her shoes.

She looked at Slocum in surprise. Slocum stood up and bowed. Novarro made the introductions.

"We seldom see North Americans here, *señor*," she said. Around her neck, suspended from a gold chain that matched her hair, was a huge emerald, as big as a walnut. Into it a snarling jaguar had been carved, with the superb, delicate artistry of the Aztecs.

Slocum's gaze was torn between the emerald and her breasts. She smiled, came close to him, and slipped his arm through the crook of her elbow.

"As a matter of fact," she continued, "we seldom see Mexicans here. Isn't that true, Basilio?"

She pressed Slocum's upper arm against her left breast. Novarro noticed it immediately, and saw Slocum looking at her breasts. He frowned.

"Basilio!"

"*Señora?*"

"I asked you a question. I shall repeat it. When do Mexicans come as guests?"

"They do not, *señora*."

"Precisely," she said with satisfaction. Turning toward Slocum, she said, "After dinner I will show you my garden. I grow English flowers in it."

"But, *señora*, he has come on business."

"Business can wait, Basilio. Don't be tiresome. Have you no manners?"

He has none, Slocum wanted to say, but remained silent, pleased with the continuing public humiliation she was putting Novarro through. Novarro flushed. He glanced quickly at Slocum, hating him for being a witness to this humiliating display of his powerlessness. Their sexual relationship, as Slocum saw, was full of insults, all done with an upper-class arrogance on her part. Not daring to respond, Novarro reacted by taking out his anger on everyone he came across—the peons in the corn fields, any strangers who might be coming by. This might even have been one of the reasons why he helped kill Wesley Putnam, Slocum began to think.

"I am sorry, *señora*. Later, then, we shall talk business."

She turned her back to Novarro. Novarro looked

at her back for an anguished moment, then shifted his hate-filled stare to Slocum. His vindictive, hostile look was so intense that Slocum could almost feel it coming off Novarro's face like steam from a radiator. So much the better. It was always easier to kill a man who hated him, Slocum felt.

Slocum turned his back on Novarro. He could not take his eyes from the emerald. He estimated its weight to be at least two ounces. Carat for carat, he knew that emeralds were worth more than diamonds. This one was worth a king's ransom. The thought came to Slocum that if he could take care of Novarro and leave with the emerald, it would cover all his expenses and pay for a ranch he knew that was for sale on the western slope of the High Sierra in northern California.

"Beautiful, isn't it?" She pulled the emerald from her décolleté and held it out toward him. "Perhaps you would like a closer look?"

Slocum bent down to look at it, but he could not resist taking a look at her breasts. She knew it and smiled secretly, and Novarro understood her motivation. He gritted his teeth.

"It *is* beautiful, *señora*," Slocum said, straightening up.

"Yes. It was part of the loot from Tenochtitlan that my husband's ancestor took in 1521. And now it is time to eat."

They entered the vast dining room. The floor was covered with red glazed tiles from Puebla. On the long oak table in the center of the room, under a chandelier blazing with candles, was a low black bowl filled with fresh violets.

"From my garden," she said proudly.

Indian servants in spotless white served them silently. Novarro angrily shoved turkey and tortillas into his mouth. He remained sullen while she probed Slocum about the city of Washington: who was the most fashionable hostess? What did she wear? What were her parties like?

Slocum invented everything. After all, he was supposed to be knowledgeable about the city. It was not too hard. He took the people he knew from his boyhood—the butcher, the postmaster, the farmer down the road—and he described them very carefully.

The specific descriptions were absolutely convincing. He was secretly amused by making the fat Mrs. Purcell, who rasised pigs on her tiny hill farm in Georgia, the wife of the French Ambassador. He kept her fat, described her accurately, but gave her a diamond tiara instead of her hairpins, which were always dropping out everywhere she went.

As for gossip, he just related the gossip of his childhood. He simply reassigned it to German princelings and English dukes.

She hung on every word. It was a world she had known years before, and no one in the state of Tamaulipas knew anything about it. She leaned forward, hanging on every word.

"At one party," Slocum recounted, "in the English embassy, the Portuguese Ambassador was so bored with the conversation of the Ambassadress that he drank champagne all through dinner rather than eat. On his left there sat the very rich wife of the English Ambassador. She had been talking to him all evening. He had not heard a word. He kept nodding, however. For dessert a large plum pudding was carried in and placed in front of her. Brandy was poured over it, it was lit, and at that moment the Portuguese Ambassador passed out, right into the plum pudding. His hair caught fire, and the Ambassadress emptied a bottle of champagne over his head, screaming, 'Have some more, you disgusting man!' A formal apology had to be delivered by her husband the next day."

Everything had happened in real life, back in Georgia. But the plum pudding had been bread pudding, the Portuguese Ambassador was Hank Prendergast, the butcher and town drunk, the champagne was applejack, and the ambassadress was Martha Vanover, whose birthday it had been.

Slocum saw that Caterina Ramirez had been drawn into the story. Novarro was becoming jealous in equal measure. Whenever he lifted his head from his plate and looked at Slocum, his eyes were filled with intense dislike.

Once Novarro tried to say something, but an imperious wave of her hand silenced him. And that, as Slocum saw plainly, made matters all the worse. When Novarro tried to speak once more, she said curtly, "*Cállate!* Shut up!" The phrase was used for rowdy children and dogs. A dull red flush suffused Novarro's face. The fact that Slocum had seen and heard everything poured acid into his brain, as Slocum plainly saw. A very slight push might well send him over the edge. Slocum hoped that she would keep her mouth shut. He did not want any violent scene until he had plotted his next step.

Luckily, she stopped her needling, which was the kind of vicious prodding husbands and wives frequently indulged in in front of guests. To Slocum it showed quite clearly that they were sleeping together.

"And what brings you to the *Hacienda de las Cinco Heridas, señor"* she asked.

In an effort to restore some sort of emotional stability to Novarro, Slocum said, with an affable nod to the *mayordomo*, "*Señor* Novarro can explain that very well, *señora*."

She turned to Novarro with an enquiring look. As he explained the reason for Slocum's visit he acquired more self-confidence. He knew horses very well, and the chance to elaborate upon his expertise made him relax his tense hostility toward Slocum.

She cut Novarro short in the middle of a sentence, waving a hand at him. "I do not care to hear all this talk of fetlocks and pasterns," she said. "Do we or do we not have the two matched bays the *señor* wants to buy?"

"Yes, *señora*," Novarro responded, with an obvious effort to control his temper.

"What pasture are they in?"

"*La Golondrina, señora.*"

"Fine. Bring them for his inspection tomorrow. In the meantime, I am very tired. *Buenas noches*, Basilio." Slocum caught an inquiring glance from Novarro and the tinest shake of her head from Caterina Ramirez. Slocum suppressed a smile; he was obviously asking if he could see her later—to screw?— and she was just as clearly telling him that the answer—for tonight, at least—was no.

She turned to Slocum. "And *buenas noches* to you, *señor*. I hope you pass a restful night."

The two men watched her walk up the stairs. Her buttocks oscillated, straining at the thin cotton fabric as she mounted. He felt his penis swell. He was sure he would not pass a restful night, just thinking about her lush, ripe figure. When he turned back to the table, Novarro was staring at him jealously. Novarro knew what he was thinking. After a few minutes of staring and refusing to enter into any conversation, Novarro abruptly stood up and walked away from the table without saying a word of farewell.

Slocum awoke when the barefoot Indian maid apologetically opened the shutters. The sun was just rising. His clothes had been cleaned and ironed during the night. He had slept well because of his exhaustion. The maid went out and came back with two more maids, who giggled as they filled the big galvanized tin tub with buckets of hot water. They placed soap and a big cotton towel over the back of a chair and withdrew. He scrubbed himself thoroughly. When he had towelled himself dry the door opened.

Caterina Ramirez stood there. She wore a silk dressing gown. She was barefoot. Her long hair hung down uncombed and still damp from her bath. She held the gown shut with one hand. She was naked underneath.

"Did you pass a restful night?" she asked.

Slocum reached for his pants. *"Sí, señora,"* he said.

"Do not bother," she said. She closed the door behind her and walked slowly toward him.

She screamed in ecstasy and pounded on his back with her heels. She made no effort to stifle her enjoyment. Although the door to the bedroom was made of solid oak planks, Slocum did not doubt that the noise she was making could be heard by anyone who might be in the hallway. Slocum knew that the story of their encounter would soon be common gossip around the Hacienda. And, sooner or later, someone trying to curry favor with Novarro would tell him about it.

But right now Slocum didn't care. In spite of the cool of the morning, she was writhing spasmodically under him with such wild energy that her skin was covered with a film of sweat. She thrust her pelvis upward to meet his downward drive with such violence that their hips met with an audible smacking noise. She was lubricating with such abandon that Slocum felt she was lined with oil. At the same time her vagina was contracting and relaxing with such vigor, milking his penis with her powerful muscles, that Slocum could not hold back any more.

He exploded inside her. She screamed with joy.

"Don't move," she said lazily.

Slocum was content just to lie on top of her with his head pillowed on her shoulder. The sheet was soaked with their sweat. The breeze filtering through the open shutters was pleasantly cool. He started once more to pull out.

"Don't."

"Aren't you going to douche?"

"No."

"No?"

"No. I want a son from you."

Slocum lay stunned.

"My husband comes home to Mexico once a year. And I am never pregnant afterwards. I think he is sterile. But one does not dare say this to a man, it is unforgivable. As for Basilio, he is only for pleasure. He made me pregnant once, but I got rid of the baby.

My husband will be here in three weeks. And then he will try once more. But it will be useless. So do not move. The boy will be tall and strong, like you. Since you and I both have green eyes, no one will wonder at it. You can get up now. But I will not move for at least an hour. I want to make sure. You understand?"

Slocum got up and took a deep breath. She spread her legs and arms wide and smiled. "And tomorrow we will do it again, *señor*."

Slocum dressed under her relaxed and amused gaze. This was a situation that had never happened to him before, and the thought that he might very well someday have a son growing up to inherit these vast spaces of Mexico stunned him.

"Are you going down for breakfast?" she asked.

He nodded.

"Just sit at the table. You will be served immediately by Teresita. She is very pretty and will probably let you know that she is available. But you are not available to anyone at the Hacienda except me. Is this understood?"

Slocum grinned and nodded.

"This is not to smile! I shall need all of you. I do not want you wasted." Then she saw his face. She hastily added, "But, of course, this is not an order. It is a favor I ask of you."

Slocum's annoyance vanished. "I grant it," he said, and walked downstairs. While he ate the freshly baked rolls and butter and drank the strong coffee Teresita had placed in front of him, the maid pressed her thigh against his leg whenever she served him. She whispered, "Do you want me tonight?"

When Slocum said, as gently as he could, *"No,*

gracias," she withdrew with an offended look. It was with relief that he saw a peon enter, remove his straw sombrero, and say, "*Señor,* the *mayordomo* has come with your horses. They are in the corral."

The horses were a lovely rich reddish brown. They looked like oiled mahogany. Novarro was sitting on the top rail watching them as they trotted nervously back and forth.

"They require training before they will pull a carriage," he said abruptly, without looking at Slocum.

"Yes, " Slocum said neutrally. He was well aware of that basic fact.

"I mention this in case you did not know."

"I appreciate your kindness," Slocum said ironically.

Novarro added, still staring at the trembling horses as they pressed nervously against the rails on the far side of the corral, "They are beautiful."

Slocum agreed.

"And they are a perfect matched pair. Everything is in proportion. They could be twins. But if they are to pull your president they will have to be castrated, of course."

Slocum opened his mouth, but Novarro interrupted. "The president of Mexico would refuse to be drawn behind two geldings, of course. But your American president lacks balls. As do all of your presidents."

Slocum resented this. It was clearly a deliberate provocation. Novarro's hand rested on his thigh, close to his gun butt. Slocum looked around quickly. No one was in sight. It was not a good time to act. Novarro would have to be killed in front of reliable witnesses who would swear that the *gringo* had killed in self-defense, and that Novarro had drawn first.

And the best witness would, of course, be Caterina Ramirez. No one would doubt her word; her statement would carry a great deal of weight.

"That is," Slocum said pleasantly, "forgive me if I say this, somewhat of a mistake. It is possible that you have not studied our history, since you are a very busy man. Being *mayordomo* of the Hacienda of the Five Wounds is a very demanding job. I suggest that, when you do have the time, you read our history. And, now, *señor*, shall we discuss price?"

Novarro was breathing harder. Slocum had not struck at the bait. He had nuzzled it gently and, like a wily trout, he had drifted away.

"Later," Novarro finally said in a choked voice. Now was the time, Slocum knew, to push the man closer to the edge. A little nudge every time they met would do the trick. But it required very precise judgment, lest Novarro go overboard too soon. The *mayordomo* jumped off the top rail and walked away. One of the *vaqueros* approached him and asked what he should do with the two horses. Novarro pushed him away so roughly that the man stumbled. This was never a wise thing to do with *vaqueros*, most of whom had independence ingrained into them. The man put his hand on his knife hilt and then removed it reluctantly. Slocum took all of this as evidence that he had better move quickly with Novarro before the man went completely out of control. He watched silently as the *vaquero* clamped his teeth tightly in rage. He tore open a bale of hay and dumped it all into the corral.

• • •

"Well, Basilio," she said briskly, "how much shall we ask?"

Slocum pushed his plate back. He had eaten a thick, rare steak, rice, and a ripe avocado made pungent with fresh lime juice from one of the hacienda's own trees.

Under the table Caterina's naked toes rubbed against Slocum's left ankle. She clasped her hands together, rested her chin on her knuckles, and leaned forward so that the emerald pendant swung in the shadow of her breasts. Novarro looked at them, then, with an effort, tore his eyes away and looked down at his plate. She turned to face Slocum, pulled up the emerald by its chain, and then began to fondle it.

"Basilio!" she said sharply.

"Ten," Novarro mumbled.

"Ten *what?*"

"Ten thousand *gringo* dollars."

"You will not use the word '*gringo*' in this house with a guest present!"

Novarro reddened. "I am sorry, *señora*," he said.

She let out an irritated sigh. She turned to Slocum and said, "Is that amount satisfactory to you, *señor?*"

Slocum had no intention of buying anything. But he had to play the game out to the end.

"Far too much, I am afraid," he said regretfully. She raised her toes till they were at his knee level. She hitched her chair closer to the table. With the added five more inches she was now able to reach as far as his genitals.

While she stroked his stiffened penis with her bare toes, she kept her elbows on the table, with her chin supported on her clasped fingers. Slocum admired her air of great calm. No one could possibly guess what she was doing under the table.

"Well, Basilio, what do you say to that?"

"Not much, *señora*. A perfect match! And he has looked everywhere for them, even in Ohio! And not found any! And they are for his president!"

"Basilio, don't shout. We can hear you."

She turned to Slocum. She was aware of the sexual warfare, and the male hostility excited her.

"What do you say to that?" she asked.

"Everything he says is true. Yet I cannot pay more than six thousand."

"Basilio?"

"Ten thousand, *señora!* Not a *centavo* less. Where else can he find them?"

"Basilio, we will talk about this later. No one is in a great hurry. The inauguration is next spring. So we will think about this overnight. Basilio, where are the horses now? In *La Golondrina?*"

"In the corral, *señora*," Novarro responded, with his usual sullen, downward stare.

"The corral! Put them in the stable immediately! And see to it that they get the best of care."

Novarro rose slowly. He had been treated for two days as if he had been a stupid child—and this not only in front of a sexual rival, but a man who was also a *gringo*.

"*Sí, señora.*"

He was still in the dining room when she turned to Slocum and said, "I shall tell the maids to prepare a bath for you. There is nothing so refreshing as a bath in the early evening. It will make you feel strong."

Slocum's penis had become hard as a result of her skilled handling.

"I shall also take one myself," she said. "I wish you *buenas noches*. On such a fine night, I believe in going to bed early."

"Of course," Slocum said. He had noticed that Novarro had paused outside the door long enough to hear her last sentence. It would be wise to be extra vigilant tonight.

She pulled off her dress and rubbed her naked breasts against Slocum's chest until her nipples hardened. One hand reached out and cupped his testicles while the other milked his penis to full, hard erection.

Slocum pulled her to his bed. She smiled and sank back on the sheet. She opened her legs wide. Her blonde triangle parted and her red lips began to gleam with moisture.

"Oh, now," she said, panting, "now, *now!* Give me a son!"

Slocum plunged deep. The door banged open behind him. Novarro stood there. He held a double-barreled shotgun. He pointed it at Slocum. *"Otro lado. hideputa!* The other side, you son of a bitch!"

"Where?" asked Slocum, with a puzzled expression. As he expected, Novarro swung the shotgun muzzle to one side, indicating the far side of the bed. In that fraction of a second Slocum shoved his hand under the pillow, pulled out his .44 and rolled over onto the floor. He landed on his knees and fired half a second before Novarro pulled both triggers. Both shotgun shells gouged out a big patch of plaster in the wall to the left of the bed. Slocum's heavy slug caught Novarro in the center of his forehead.

The combination of the shock of the impact and the recoil of the shotgun forced Novarro to stagger backward into the hallway. He fell back. The shotgun clattered at his feet.

The acrid smell of cordite filled the room. She said tersely, "Get dressed." By the time he had pulled on his clothes and boots she had slipped her dress on and combed her hair into order with her fingers. Three wide-eyed maids appeared.

"Have him taken to his house," she ordered. "Clean up this mess. Tell Gregorio to come here."

She turned to Slocum. "I am sorry that this happened. Perhaps it would be best to postpone our discussion about the horses." She mused while she watched the maids mop up the bloodstains.

"Señora!"

"Ah, Gregorio. Ride to Linares. Tell the sheriff that Basilio was drunk, and that he attacked my guest, who then defended himself. I shall bury Basilio. There is no need for the sheriff to come here. The next time I happen to be in Linares I will go to see him and give him all the details. But now I am too busy. Is this clear?"

"Si, señora."

"You may go." She turned to Slocum. "There will be no problems. The sheriff will do as I say. Tomorrow shall we discuss the business of the horses?"

"As you wish."

"Until then."

But Slocum decided there was no point in staying. After all, his business at the Hacienda was finished. So at lunch he told her that the price demanded was far more than he could pay.

She smiled. "It doesn't matter," she said. "I think

your visit will prove profitable to me. Yes, I am sure it will."

"I also," Slocum replied. "It has been most useful."

He had thought of taking the emerald with him, but he finally decided against it. There was no way he would take away part of his son's inheritance. Moreover, if she found out it had disappeared with him, a fast rider to the sheriff at Linares could make things very difficult for him in Mexico. And she had smoothed his path by her offhand message to the sheriff. No, no emerald.

When he reached the place in the Hacienda road where it swung west to Linares he turned for a last look. She had climbed to his room and he could see her standing in the window. She blew him a goodbye kiss and closed the shutters.

7

Slocum turned in his buggy at Linares and got back his deposit. He counted all his cash as he sat in a nearby cantina. It came to a hundred and five dollars and sixty-five cents. It was simply not enough to pay for the remainder of the traveling he had to do in Mexico. He regretted for a moment not taking Caterina Ramirez's emerald, but he soon put that thought away. He needed to make a withdrawal somewhere, and to do it in Mexico would be too risky.

The best way to get it would be to go to the States, make his withdrawal, and then immediately cross the border back into Mexico. That would so complicate the problem of pursuit that whatever he got could be considered a gift from the gods. He ordered a bottle of fine Mexican beer and sipped it as he considered what to do.

By the time he had finished his second bottle of beer he knew what to do. He paid his bill and retraced his steps to Brownsville, first making sure he knew the exact train schedule for the trains leaving Matamoros. It developed that the train on which he arrived at 11:10 A.M. would be leaving that same afternoon at 2:15. Both the conductor and the engineer were Americans. Slocum walked up to the engine and got into conversation with the engineer, a lanky Texan named Jack Perkins.

"Train's leavin' at two-fifteen?" he called up to the engineer.

"Yeah."

"I know these greaser trains," Slocum said. "All right if I come by about two forty-five? There's a gal I want to see in Brownsville and she might not want me to leave so soon."

"When Jack Perkins is at the throttle, two-fifteen is two-fifteen, pardner," Perkins said. "No matter what happens elsewhere in the Raypooblica, Perkins leaves on time. Got that?" He sounded indignant, Slocum was happy to note.

"Got that," Slocum said.

"What's your line?" Perkins asked.

"Hardware. I carry sample cases around. Mighty heavy to drag around. Couldn't wait ten minutes extra for me, could you?"

"Not even for Jesus Christ hisself," Perkins said proudly. "Me 'n' my conductor run the only on-time train in this goddamn country, *seguro!* It ain't much of a train, but it runs on time, by God!"

Slocum rented a horse at a livery stable near the train yards. He rode it across to Brownsville and tied the horse at the hitching rack near the Merchants' and Farmers' Bank. He walked down the block and had a shave and a haircut and had his boots well shined. He next dropped into a saddle-and-luggage shop and bought a sturdy secondhand leather valise. Then he turned around and walked back to the bank. He paused for a moment in front of it while he remembered what that bank had done to him.

Five years before, the bank had foreclosed on a mortgage it held on a four-thousand-acre spread Slocum owned. He was running about six hundred head of fine stock. A combination of screw-worm, blue northers, and a two-year drought had wiped him out. He could have made it all right if the bank would have gone easy on him, because the next year it rained a lot, and everyone else in the area did well. But Avery, the banker, had said no.

Henry Avery was the bank president. He had been a colonel in the Fifth Illinois, and when he found out that Slocum had fought throughout the War as a Confederate cavalryman, that had killed the loan extension.

In his back pocket Slocum had stored away three lengths of leather thongs he had picked up in the leather shop. When he walked into the bank wearing his fine broadcloth suit and carrying his fine leather valise with brass fittings, he looked like a prosperous businessman. When he asked to see Avery, he was ushered in immediately. He sat down in the comfortable armchair across from Avery's desk. The chair was reserved for important clients.

Avery did not recognize the struggling rancher of five years before. Slocum had put on a little weight, but he had more lines in his face. Moreover, he was clean-shaven, and looked so well-to-do that Avery made no connection whatsoever.

"What can I do for you, Mr.—"

"Grant."

"Mr. Grant?"

Slocum smiled, pulled out his .44, placed it on his lap, and pointed it at Avery's stomach. "Do what I tell you. Call in the head teller. First, give me a loan agreement and a pen."

Avery's eyes bulged.

"The loan agreement, please," Slocum reminded him politely.

Avery handed it to him.

"Thank you," Slocum said. "When the teller comes in, give him my valise and tell him to put in four hundred double eagles." Mexicans did not like paper money.

Slocum had tested the handles on the valise. They were solidly constructed. The weight of the gold wouldn't pull them off.

"Now, when the teller comes in, no secret signs, no winking, nothing like that, " Slocum said softly. "If you do, I'll blow a hole in your belly big enough for a blind man to piss through. I've got this .44 under the loan agreement pointing just right. Hop to it."

One look at Slocum's hard, merciless eyes convinced Avery that he had better hop to it.

When the teller entered, he saw a relaxed rancher filling out a loan application. Avery too looked relaxed, since he was leaning back with his arms folded, the way Slocum had told him to.

"Wagner," Avery said, "put four hundred double eagles in this, please."

Wagner hesitated. "Wouldn't the gentleman want to count them first?"

"The gentleman trusts y'all."

At that point Avery suddenly recognized Slocum. Wagner, flattered at the trust placed in him, walked out with the valise. Avery nervously began tapping his fingers on the desk.

"Lean back, friend," Slocum said.

When Wagner came back, his arm showed the strain of the weight.

"Thank you," Slocum said gravely. Wagner left.

Slocum took out the rawhide thongs. He tied Avery's wrists, then his ankles. He tied the ankles firmly to one of the desk legs so that Avery could not bang them against the floor to attract attention. He tied Avery's handkerchief into his mouth for a gag, and used the same thong to make his head fast to the other desk leg. Avery could not bang his head. His wrists were tied to his belt, so no movement there was possible.

Satisfied, Slocum picked up the valise. "Thanks for the loan," Slocum said. "I had to wait five years for it, but it's sure worth it." He hefted the valise, walked to the door, opened it, and, turning around, said loudly enough for Wagner to hear, "Once more, Mr. Avery, thanks for the loan."

He closed the door and walked through the bank. Wagner, flattered because the new customer had trusted his count, waved a cheerful goodbye. Slocum nodded, mounted his horse, rode north a few blocks, turned right when he was out of sight of the bank, and headed south once more toward Matamoros. He dropped off the horse and walked to the train. He was not too surprised to see that the train left exactly when Perkins said it would, ten minutes after he boarded.

Slocum rode the train to Monterrey; there he changed to the more elaborate one for Mexico City. He bought a pair of canvas pants and a canvas jacket, such as a mining expert might wear who would be looking around for a likely prospect for future exploitation. He picked up a geologist's pick and hammer in the Thieves' Market—*La Lagunilla*. Satisfied, he took the next train for Cuernavaca.

There he acquired a small hammock, a handful of tortillas, three hard-boiled eggs, and two mangoes. He rented a horse at a livery stable near the train station and then set out for Taxco, fifty miles south, high up in the mountains of Guerrero.

He rode along a valley filled with corn fields. In the distance there rose worn volcanic peaks. Late that afternoon, he began climbing into the mountains. The air was filled with pungent smoke made by the charcoal burners' fires. A few miles before he decided it would be time to stop for the night and sling his hammock, he passed by five white-clad peasants who were cutting corn stalks in a mountain field with their razor-sharp machetes. He waved. There was no response from the usually friendly *campesinos*.

He kept climbing the winding, twisting road. For much of its length a creek ran beside it. The water was clear and cold. *Ahuehuete* trees—much like American willows—lined the banks. When it grew darker the charcoal-burners' fires starred the dark mountain faces like rubies. He made a halt for the night. He slung his hammock between two tree trunks.

He ate the eggs and the tortillas and, peeling the mangoes, he ate the delicious orange-colored flesh. He washed his hands in the water and lay back in the hammock. He couldn't sleep. Somewhere in the mountains Hector Ruiz—the third man—was sleeping. But it would not be easy to find him.

The smoke made by the *carboneros'* fires was pungent and acrid, yet not unpleasant. Slocum rolled a *cigarillo*. He was smoking it, arms clasped behind his head and looking up at the stars, when he suddenly heard a *clink*. The noise was made by something stepping on a stone in the edges of the creekbed and forcing it against another stone.

He pulled the Colt from its holster and let one arm hang down as if he were asleep. There was some more clinking. With that noise, it was probably not a *tigre*. Jaguars moved as silently as house cats. He began a light snore.

Five figures in white rose silently from the creekbed and stood outlined against the red glows of the charcoal fires. Slocum saw the firelight glinting from their sharp machete blades. Five was the number of the silent *campesinos* he had ridden past early that evening. Too much for coincidence.

It was clear to Slocum: they had noticed him. He was a stranger and well-dressed. There would be no blood feuds. They had taken a short cut through mountain paths and had followed the creekbed till they saw his *cigarillo* end glowing in the dark.

They were twenty-five feet away. He gave them one last chance.

"*Quien vive?* Who's there?" he asked sleepily. No one answered. Suddenly the leader shouted "*Ahora!*" They began to run at the hammock with their machetes raised high, ready for the terrible downward stroke. If it were not for the poor light, Slocum would have aimed at their legs.

But now he could not take that chance. He shot three of them in the stomach. The remaining two faltered. Slocum held his fire. *"Somos cobardes?"* yelled one of the two remaining upright. He ran toward Slocum. Slocum put his fourth bullet in the man's stomach. The fifth man broke and scrambled frantically down the slope to the creekbed. Slocum heard him running and falling, running and falling.

Slocum reloaded and waited. The four men were moaning in agony. Slocum was still in the hammock. The *cigarillo* was still burning in his mouth. He straddled the hammock and swung a leg over. He turned to unhitch the hammock from the trees. As he began to roll it up, he heard a clink of steel on stone. One of the men was crawling toward him, one hand pressed against his stomach. The other hand was pulling the machete along behind him. Slocum did not want to kill him. He bent down and chopped him hard on the side of his neck. The man went down flat and remained motionless.

Slocum finished rolling the hammock. The horse was still grubbing for grass blades, somewhat nervous because it had smelled blood. Slocum shoved the hammock into the saddlebag on top of the gold. He mounted, reached the road, and continued on his way to Taxco in the darkness. If the men did not bleed to death they would die of peritonitis. A bad way to die, Slocum thought, but then they would not have hesitated to slice him to death with their machetes. He let his horse amble at its own pace the rest of the night while the acrid smell of the burning wood filled the night winds. He kept his hand on his gun butt. The road became very narrow at times, and ambushes were easy. This was not a country that was friendly to strangers.

8

Taxco had once been a silver capital. Now, its mines stripped of their precious metal, the little hillside town dozed sleepily away. The narrow, steep streets of the town, a hundred miles south of Mexico City, were laid with cobblestones. The houses had roofs of red tiles. Narrow, steep canyons called *barrancas* sliced through Taxco in every direction. Skinny dogs prowled the *barrancas* nosing for scraps of garbage. The dogs slept most of the day and howled endlessly all night long.

Slocum found a *fonda* close to the tree-shaded plaza. The horse was stabled adequately in the back. People were honest in small towns, Slocum had discovered, so he had no hesitation in dumping his saddlebags on the bed. He knew the Indian servants would not touch them.

He washed and went out to secure information.

People looked at him in friendly curiosity. On the second floor of a building that overlooked the plaza he found a good restaurant. It faced the beautiful seventeenth-century church built of pink volcanic stone from the great profits of the silver mines.

He told the proprietor of the restaurant, Don Pascual, that he was a mining engineer who had come to Taxco to see if it would pay to open up new silver mines in the surrounding mountains.

"Indeed," said Don Pascual, "the church opposite was built with silver money. Hence its gorgeous carvings, the gold leaf, the great candlesticks, the carved altar. They quarried *tezontle* so that it would always look like a healthy girl just out of the bath." He sighed. "But they took out all the silver, I am afraid. Others have come and given up the search. There is none left, I assure you. I say this with regret, *señor*. The town is poor, but remembers its glory."

"There may be some silver yet."

"I doubt it, *señor*."

"Where there is life, there are possibilities."

"To this I have no objections. Do you seriously think you may find something? If you do, it would be a great thing for this poor town."

"In the States there are many clever inventors."

"I have heard this. It is clearly true."

"They have a new way of searching for precious metals."

"Ah?"

"More I cannot say," Slocum said regretfully.

"I understand. And you are here for that purpose?"

Slocum smiled and said nothing. Dom Pascual said that Slocum must be his guest for the next drink. Slocum accepted. It was clear that all Taxco—and a day or so later all of the surrounding countryside—would know that there was an American engineer searching for silver. This would permit Slocum to move around without provoking too much curiosity.

Afterward, Slocum went back to his room. He was tired and he had slept very little the night before. He dozed during the afternoon, ate in the dining room for dinner, and then went upstairs and slept again. The barking of the dogs disturbed him a little, but he soon adjusted to it, and slept all through their nighttime howling.

A bougainvillea vine, hundreds of years old, writhed around the iron balcony railing outside his room. When he woke up in the morning, hummingbirds were flickering in and out of the vine. The air at this altitude was like wine. It was hard to believe that in his search to kill Hector Ruiz he had killed four men almost incidentally.

He washed and shaved. He hung up his good clothes in the wardrobe. After he ate breakfast he went back to his room, buckled on his Colt, and taking the geologist's hammer and two sacks for ore samples, he visited the cook. She made him two sandwiches from tortillas and fried ham. She had already heard about his purpose in coming to Taxco, and she wished him good luck.

He shoved the sandwiches in the pockets of his canvas jacket—good water was no problem in the mountains—and walked to the hill overlooking Taxco. The mountains sprawled everywhere. He had no idea where to go to look for Ruiz, but the view westward was pleasant, so he walked west. The road soared upward.

From time to time he crawled up a steep, barren hillside and hacked away at rocky outcrops with his hammer. Although he saw no one, he was sure that he was being observed by someone. When the sun was directly overhead he sat on the edge of the road with his legs dangling in space and ate his tortillas and ham.

A *zapilote* floating on a thermal let himself be lifted up from the valley floor far below till he was parallel with Slocum. Then the scavenger bird with the cruel hooked beak kept himself soaring, almost motionless, while he twisted his naked red neck to stare at the human. Feathers at the ends of his eight-foot wing spread flicked up and down as they controlled his motionless hover. The bird's eyes were pitiless.

"I'm hunting a bit myself," said Slocum. He tossed a piece of ham into space. The *zapilote* tilted, folded his wings, and fell like a stone. He caught the meat and soared upward once more.

"Maybe I'll get lucky too," Slocum said. The problem was how to find Hector Ruiz without his finding out that someone was looking for him. Slocum did not know what he looked like or even how old he was, or what he did for a living.

He sat after dinner and watched the crowd saunter around the plaza below while he thought about what to do next. Someone in the plaza was playing a lovely melody on a marimba.

"Beautiful, no?" It was Don Pascual.

"Clearly."

"May I join you?"

"*Con mucho gusto.*"

Don Pascual ordered a round of beer. "You are my guest," he said.

"I am honored."

"No, it is I who am honored to talk to someone who has been farther than Cuernavaca. Many people in this town have not even been there, and it is not far! I have. I have even gone to Mexico City; this is a large distance."

"That it is."

"Forgive me if I intrude on your thoughts, but have you had any luck?"

Slocum had determined upon a plan. Now Don Pascual, in his eager questioning, had provided the means.

"Yes, yes. I think so," Slocum replied.

"Marvelous!"

"Yes, I think it will pay us to open a few exploratory shafts. I have found signs of silver ore in many places. And there are new chemical methods—cheap ones, you understand—which will enable us to extract silver easily from its various compounds."

"*Excelente!* There will be much work for *Taxqueños*, then?"

"Without doubt."

"What marvelous news! *Mesero!*" he called out to the waiter. *Dos cervezas!* We shall drink to the success of the new mines!"

Slocum put a hand on Don Pascual's forearm.

"Softly, softly," he said. "If the news gets around too soon, too many people will come here to look for work. Crime rates will go up, speculators in land and houses and lumber will appear. Why should not the people of Taxco be the ones to benefit?"

"I understand," Don Pascual said, almost in a whisper. He placed a forefinger beside his nose. "Softly, softly, catches the monkey, it is said."

"Very true. Who should be the first to benefit?"

"The people of Taxco," Don Pascual said. He was almost in a hypnotic state as he fantasized the rain of silver pesos which would be falling on Taxco and also into his pockets.

"Absolutely. Before I came here," Slocum said casually, "I was given a list of people who would be hired in supervisory capacities. People with roots in Taxco. People who would want the mines to be a long-range success. We do not want men who drift from job to job. Such people do not have their hearts in their work and care nothing for the towns where they have their temporary habitation."

"This is clearly true. You phrase it well." Don Pascual was fascinated.

"But," Slocum said, "we do not know if this is a good list. We must know more about these people: their age, health, their attitude toward work, their experience, where they live, whether they can be trusted—"

"Indeed! This is very sensible. I have heard it said that an English general, or Draque, the great pirate, once said there were only three rules for managing an army—*pay well, command well, hang well*. It is so in everything, *señor*, even in my small establishment."

"That is very well phrased, Don Pascual," Slocum said, with an admiring look. No one despises flattery, and the Mexican beamed.

"So," Slocum went on, "here is our list." Fourth

from the top he had written the name of Hector Ruiz. He placed the list on the table in front of Don Pascual.

"We realize that this will take quite a lot of your time to work on this," Slocum said. "And so we will pay well."

"This I cannot permit."

"Ah, but permit me to remind you of your quote from the English general."

Don Pascual chuckled.

"We will pay well for accurate details. And we are not cheap." Slocum placed a gold double eagle on the table. Don Pascual's eyes widened. "This will be for your first day's work."

"It is too much, *señor!*"

It was, but Slocum said, "Not for accuracy, and, above all, secrecy."

"Secrecy?"

"It would not be good for word to get around. A wild rush to Taxco would be the result."

"Yes. Yes, I can understand that."

"So, accuracy and secrecy. And, above all, no haste."

Don Pascual liked that.

"Three, four, five days—take as long as you need. Each day I will give you one gold double eagle."

Don Pascual beamed.

Slocum spent the next day knocking chunks of rock from rocky outcrops and sticking them into his ore bags. In the evening he returned to the *fonda,* saw that his horse was well fed, went up to his room, bathed, changed, ate dinner, and then strolled up the cobblestone street to Don Pascual's bar.

As soon as he sat down the Mexican joined him. "I have found out about the first six on your list, *señor*," he said proudly.

"Excellent!" Slocum put out his hand.

Don Pascual said, with embarrassment, "It is with shame that I announce that writing is difficult for me. But, in compensation, God has given me a good memory. Shall I proceed?"

"One moment. Give me the list. I must write down what you tell me, since it must go to my office in San Francisco." Don Pascual found a pencil stub in his cash drawer.

"First," Don Pascual said softly. "Manuel Ortiz. He is thirty two years old, *mas o menos*, more or less. He had a broken left ankle, and walks with a slight limp. He owns a *carniceria* on the road to Ixcateopan. He is not very intelligent, but he is completely honest."

Slocum pretended to listen carefully. He made notes on his list. He made notes on Armando Menendez and Domingo Cespedes.

"Next. Hector Ruiz. Ah, this is a bad one! But there is a happy ending!"

"Why?" Slocum's heart speeded up, but he kept his face calm.

"Permit me to tell you." Like most people who cannot read, Don Pascual delighted in the art of oral narrative, with its dramatic pauses to heighten suspense.

"He would be about thirty. Thin. Strong. Oh, yes, very intelligent. The priest here at Santa Prisca liked him and sent him off to a seminary in Guadalajara. There he got into a fight with a fellow student. With a knife! Imagine that! In a seminary!" Don Pascual shook his head at the evildoing. He crossed himself.

"Then, of course, he was expelled. Then he went north."

"North?"

"To Sonora. At the seminary he had read much of our history. So he became angry at the *norteamericanos*—with your permission, *señor*—and wanted to fight them. For a time he was with General Cortina in Tamaulipas, but when the Texas Rangers killed a lot of them, he went farther along the border, to Arizona. There he joined a general named Duran and fought many valiant battles against the soldiers of the American army in Arizona. This I know because of the letters he wrote to his mother. She took them to the priest to be read, and the priest came here to drink sometimes and to talk about Spain, where he comes from."

If Ruiz wanted to glorify his exploits with that murderer Duran in his letters to the home folks, it gave grim amusement to Slocum.

"Then?" he asked.

"Then he came back here, about two months ago."

That would be about the time that Slocum had killed Duran in Magdalena.

"Why did he come back?"

"It is not known. He was suddenly very nervous."

"I see. And where does he live in Taxco?"

Don Pascual smiled and held up his forefinger in a gently chiding way, as if to say, *Have patience, I am telling a good story and must be allowed to tell it my way.*

"So he went away. He clearly wanted to hide from something or someone, for some reason. I personally think there was something in a recent letter—the postmaster tells me he received a letter recently—that made him want to do this. He went to the tiny village of San Andres Acatlán, where there are only a few *campesinos*. This is about twenty miles north of here, and of course, a stranger appearing there would be noticed immediately."

"I see. And is he there now?"

Don Pascual's smile grew broader. "Yes, one can say that."

"Where does he live?"

Don Pascual let out a bark of delighted laughter.

"In the cemetery!" he gasped with amusement.

Slocum's startled face made the Mexican laugh even louder. When he had recovered he said, "I beg your pardon, *señor,* but did I not tell the story well?"

"Yes, you did. How did he die? Out of curiosity."

"In order to eat, this man who could both read and write and had travelled much became a *campesino!* Three nights ago he and four other simple fools attacked a horseman on the Cuernavaca road in order to rob him and sell his horse and saddle. This was Ruiz's idea, so you can see he was a bad choice for your list. The horseman was an extraordinary man. He shot four of them when they thought he was asleep. Three have died and one is dying and the *curandera* says she is helpless. He is in great pain. And Hector Ruiz is, as I have said, in the cemetery near San Andres Acatlán. There. You can cross *him* off your list."

Slocum stared at the list.

"I do not know who put his name on the list, *señor.* Tell them they were badly advised," Don Pascual went on.

"Yes, I will." He took the pencil stub and drew a line through Ruiz's name.

"Is this not the strange working of God?" Don Pascual demanded. "Ruiz was running away from his fate, and he ran right into it, just the same."

"God is good," Slocum said heavily, and rose. Don Pascual gave him a startled look. Slocum put a double eagle on the table. "For your fine work. You have saved us much trouble."

"Many thanks. Tomorrow I will have more information for you."

Slocum stood up. "I find that I must leave today. A sudden realization." He pulled out three more double eagles. "This will cover your time for the rest of the list. I shall be back in a month."

Don Pascual stood up. They shook hands. He said, "It has been a pleasure, *señor*." Slocum nodded and lifted a hand in farewell. One more to go.

He could not have known that the last one would be the most hazardous of all.

9

Alejandro Robles was the fourth man.

All that Slocum knew was that Robles could be found somewhere in the mountainous area of the western Sierra Madre range, near the town of Tlaltenango. Nothing more than that.

So the first step would be to go to Tlaltenango. A map would be useful, but maps were very hard to find in Mexico. Mexico City would be the best place to find one. Slocum got on the train at Cuernavaca. He got off in Mexico City, after the train had puffed its way over the ten-thousand-foot circle of mountains surrounding the city.

He took a room in the Hotel Orizaba, close to the

station. Since the gold coins were too heavy, he changed half of them into U. S. fifty-dollar bills. These he inserted into his money belt.

There was no place in the city that sold maps. Apparently the government feared that the maps would be used by unfriendly armies planning military campaigns. After all, there had been a war with Texas, then one with the United States, only a little over thirty years before; and more recently the French, in order to support the doomed Emperor Maximilian, had invaded Mexico and had suffered a decisive defeat in Puebla. The emperor had been shot by a firing squad at Queretaro, not far from where Slocum intended to go. The emperor's crown jewels and most of his personal treasure had disappeared at the time.

Of course, with typical Mexican inconsistency, the maps were available at the Biblioteca Nacional. The librarian had been surprised, then pleased, with Slocum's excellent Spanish. He complimented him.

"You are very kind," Slocum said. He found Tlaltenango. The village was thirty miles or so northeast of San Felipe. And San Felipe—although it made no impression on Slocum at the time—was about sixty miles northwest of Queretaro, where Maximilian had been shot, and from where the treasure had vanished.

The librarian was watching over Slocum's shoulder with great interest. People very seldom came into his department and he welcomed conversation.

"Your business takes you there?" he asked.

Slocum nodded.

"That is unfortunate," the librarian said with a frown.

Slocum shrugged.

"Life is full of unfortunate events," he said. This time around, he had decided to be a geologist. Such people could move anywhere without exciting suspicion. "On the contrary, however," he went on, "I find it most fortunate to be a geologist, particularly in your large, beautiful country, with its varied mineral deposits."

"Thank you," the librarian said. "However, I used the word 'unfortunate' because of a man named Alejandro Robles."

An electric shock went through Slocum. He kept his face calm as he carefully folded the map and returned it to the librarian.

"Robles?" Slocum asked, with a puzzled look.

"My brother has a small ranch not too far from San Felipe. This is close to Tlaltenango. It is to San Felipe that Robles goes from time to time to buy salt, ammunition, women. On his way there he kills one or two of my brother's cattle. His men eat them right there. My brother is a brave man, but he has a wife and several young children. He has to be careful, you understand?"

"Of course, I take it you do not care for this Robles."

"Although I am over fifty, I would like to go there and kill this animal. But he would kill me. And I, too, have a wife and many children to support." The man's coat was threadbare, Slocum saw. Public officials were badly paid in Mexico.

"So, *señor,* in your search for minerals, stay away from San Felipe, and especially avoid Tlaltenango. Robles would kill you just for your fine boots. Perhaps not for mine, but for yours, definitely yes."

"And they are old boots, too. Thank you for this

information. But I will take my chances with this Robles person."

"Not 'person.' *Animal.*"

At San Felipe there was only one *fonda*. A high wall surrounded it; broken glass was set in the top. In the patio of the *fonda* a long table was placed under the trees. Slocum ate there. His room had shutters. He slept on a cot. Pegs jutting out of the whitewashed wall held his belongings. Aside from the occasional smear left by someone smashing a cockroach with a shoe, the place was clean.

"Robles is an animal."

Animals—particularly the dangerous ones—had to be stalked with enormous patience. Slocum lit a *cigarillo* and thought while he sat at the dinner table at the end of his second day in San Felipe. He had strolled around the first day, wanting to give people the impression that he was in no hurry, that he knew what he was doing, and that he was willing to live at the tempo Mexicans had adopted for themselves. The town was small, but it had a plaza with trees and iron benches. Slocum sat on a bench and drank watermelon juice and smiled at the children at play. He was exhibiting patience while he planned his next moves.

At the other end of the table there sat a large, fat cattle buyer who wore a pearl-handled .45 in a holster. It had been Slocum's experience that men who wore elaborate and expensive guns were usually bad shots. Next to the fat man was a thin, pale priest who never took his eyes from his plate.

The lowest branch of the tree under which they were sitting stretched horizontally above the table. A kerosene lamp hung from it. Moths fluttered around its strong yellow glow. The cattle buyer, who was named Lucas Carrizo, was boasting of his shrewd purchases from the ranchers in the area. He had made a lot of good buys around Tlaltenango, he said.

Slocum began to listen, although his face showed no change of expression.

Carrizo said that the ranchers were desperate because of the raids of a certain Robles. So, he said, they sold their cattle cheaply, because they would rather take very little for them than lose everything.

"He can fire a Winchester so rapidly," Carrizo said, "that four or five empty shells from the ejector are in the air at the same time, falling at different heights to the ground."

Someone expressed skepticism.

"Not only that," Carrizo went on, in his overbearing way, "he can take a Colt in each hand, set up a playing card sixty feet away, and put all twelve bullets in the card fast, *fast!*"

The priest was not impressed with stories of marksmanship. He was waiting for his replacement to come up from San Luis Tuxtla. He said suddenly, his eyes downcast, as if he were a young nun, "This is a very interesting area. Historically, that is."

"Nonsense," the cattle buyer said crisply. "Here and in the Sierra there were Indians. But the Spaniards quickly killed most of them. Made them work themselves to death in the mines."

The priest was a Spaniard. He blushed.

Carrizo went on. "And in the War for Independence—from *Spain*—" Here the priest blushed again. "There was not even a single skirmish here in San Felipe. It was not even worth fighting over! All that happens here is that people make babies, grow corn, breed a few cattle, drink *pulque*, cut each other with machetes, and grow corn."

The priest waited patiently for a chance to talk.

"Nevertheless," he said softly, "here is where they brought the treasure of Maximilian." He waved a hand at the mountains to the east.

The cattle buyer was from Durango and had never heard of the treausre. He said, with an air of amused cynicism, "I have never heard of this so-called treasure."

"Oh, yes," the priest said gently. "There were crown jewels and necklaces, and rings. And chests of gold coins, all sorts of things. It was the imperial treasure, you see, and it went wherever Maximilian went. So, after the *pobrecito* was shot, the treasure was put on mules, in charge of a captain, and suddenly the mule train was attacked. If I bore you, please tell me."

"On the contrary, Father," Slocum said. This talk of treasure in Robles's stamping ground was beginning to give him an idea. Lucas Carrizo grunted skeptically, but was silent.

"Many soldiers were killed," the priest went on. "The others disappeared. It is thought that the captain had persuaded half his men to join him in seizing the treasure. At the signal, the traitors killed the loyal soldiers. Then they rode north from Queretaro, with the mules, to somewhere east of San Felipe." Here the priest pointed into the mountains that rimmed San Felipe.

"Somewhere in there he found a cave. He put the treasure inside, walled it up with stones and mortar, and that night, when the soldiers were numb from exhaustion, the captain said he would stand guard while they slept. Grateful, they immediately fell asleep.

He killed them all, one by one, with his knife. Then he rode away to wait for better times."

"What happened to him?" Carrizo asked, interested in spite of his doubt.

"Oh," said the priest, "the people say that his conscience gave him no rest. So one night he killed himself."

Carrizo said with a sneer, "If there were no witnesses, how is all this about the killing in the cave known? Hey?"

"The Indians saw it. They see everything in the mountains, you understand. Eventually one of them, a devout *cristiano*, told Father Demetrio, who later told me. It is true, my friend."

"Where's the map?" demanded Carrizo with a grin.

The priest was bewildered. "There is no map," he said.

"Come on, Father," Carrizo said in his jeering tone that Slocum had come to despise. "You must have it with you. The captain gave it to you on his deathbed when you gave him absolution on the condition that he tell you where the treasure was hidden."

He turned to Slocum and winked. The priest was pale. Humor of this type confused and embarrassed him. He looked down at his plate.

Slocum leaned forward and tapped Carrizo on the shoulder. "Apologize," he said, so softly that the priest did not hear him.

"Chinga tu madre!" After he had delivered this most obscene and insulting of Mexican curses, Carrizo turned his back to Slocum. The priest blushed violently.

"Now you will have to apologize to me as well," Slocum said.

Carrizo was used to bullying people with his size, and with the confidence that his bulk gave him.

"Enough!" Carrizo said, and, turning to face Slocum, he reached for the ivory butt of his Colt. Slocum grabbed Carrizo's wrist, reversed it so that the elbow joint locked, and then pushed hard on the elbow. Carrizo's head slammed against the table top. All conversation stopped.

The priest was rigid. *"Señores, señores,"* he whispered.

Carrizo's face was pressed flat against the table. He could not break the iron grip at his elbow. He turned his head sideways and glared up at Slocum. It was the face of a mad dog.

Carrizo was a brave man and a hard man. Anyone who carried money with which to buy cattle and who traveled through that wild part of Mexico by himself had to be brave. But when he saw Slocum's eyes, cold and pitiless like a predator's, he said quickly, "Father, I beg your pardon. And yours too, *señor*."

The priest was now red with embarrassment. Slocum released Carrizo's arm and straightened up. "Good night, Father."

The priest mumbled, "Good night, my son." He could not meet Slocum's hard green eyes.

Slocum washed and got in his cot. He clasped his hands behind his head and thought that for someone trying to pass unnoticed, he was making a goddamn mess out of it. He tried to sleep, but it was no use. He sat up, lit a *cigarillo*, and tried to figure out how to find Robles.

And around three in the morning he had his answer. It was simple. He did not have to try to find Robles, because Robles was going to look for him with great seriousness. Slocum would be the bait.

The first item on the agenda was to tell people that he was a geologist. He was looking for valuable minerals, he would tell anyone who asked. But not necessarily gold and silver. Copper and lead would do nicely. Or even sulphur.

But he would be doing his searching in such a way that people would not believe him. People tended to be suspicious of strangers. In this case, this quality would play into Slocum's hands.

He hoped.

In the morning Slocum waited in his room until he saw Carrizo ride out. Slocum did not want to risk an encounter with the man. If he were to kill Carrizo, things would become very complicated with the *alguacil*. Mexican jails were unpleasant places, and twice as bad for *gringos*. Slocum could well imagine the *alguacil* saying regretfully that the tall green-eyed *gringo* was, unfortunately, shot while attempting to escape. Carrizo would have, without question, very good relations with the various government officials. Best to be careful and be sensible for a change.

He went into the courtyard, sat at the table, and drank the strong Mexican black coffee and ate two hard rolls, freshly baked.

The proprietor asked him how he had slept.

"Very well, *gracias*. Would you know where I can buy a burro?"

He would need one to carry his supplies in his role of geologist.

"To ride, *señor*?"

The man was not joking. Many people preferred the intelligent, sure-footed burro to horses for riding narrow mountain trails.

"No. To carry equipment."

"Ah, Of course." He paused, then he added, *"Con su permiso, señor*—what equipment?"

Slocum said, "The equipment I am going to bring from Mexico City. I shall be leaving now. But when I return, in two or three days, I would like a good burro at a fair price."

"This can be arranged."

"Good." Slocum paid him and left for Mexico City. His reason for going there was to go to a market behind the cathedral. There a man named Guillermo Sandoval kept a little shop which supplied certain things to the devout Indians who had come—some on their knees all the way—from their villages to beg favors from *La Morena*—the Brown Virgin. Her life-sized statue was covered with rubies, emeralds, pearls, and diamonds, and stood inside the great cathedral.

If their prayers were answered, many of the devout wanted to adorn their own Virgins in their tiny churches in their villages the same way. Since real jewels were out of the question, Sandoval did a good business in selling the Indians jewels made of colored glass. The Virgin, after all, as he told the Indians, was certainly not a jewelry expert. She would take the will for the deed. She would be flattered by the fact they had brought her a gift all the way from Mexico City. And after all, he added persuasively, what else mattered?

Slocum bought a handful each of Sandoval's emeralds, rubies, and diamonds.

Y perlas? And pearls?"

He held up a pearl the size of a cherry pit. In bad

light, a man like Robles might think that the diamonds or rubies were real, but the pearls were obviously crude fakes.

"No pearls."

"The *Indios* will never know if they're real. They love them."

Slocum shook his head and slipped his purchases into a pocket. He might have found all these fake jewels closer to San Felipe than Mexico City, but the danger of being spotted there by coincidence was too much to risk.

Next, Slocum dropped in at the Thieves' Market. A man could find anything he wanted there; if he could not, a simple statement of what was needed into a dealer's ear would guarantee its arrival in one or two days.

He told the dealer in plumber's and carpenter's tools that he was looking for a portable chemical testing kit such as geologists carry. The dealer had never heard of such a thing, but he simply nodded and remarked, "Probably tomorrow morning, *señor*."

"*Hasta la mañana*."

"*Hasta la mañana, señor*."

Slocum spent the rest of the day reading geological texts in the *Biblioteca Nacional*. He picked up some valuable information.

The same librarian was there and remembered him. "Have you been to Tlaltenango?" he asked with interest.

"No," Slocum said. "I took your advice and decided to stay out of danger. I have been examining the prospects near Oaxaca."

This was about three hundred miles south of San Felipe.

"Excellent decision! They are peaceful people down there. And they grow oranges."

"I like oranges," Slocum said. One never knew whether gossip about his visit to San Felipe might spread from the librarian who, bored at his job, would start a conversation with anyone. And the long arm of coincidence might operate to Slocum's disadvantage. Once Slocum knew someone who had robbed a bank in Syracuse, grabbed fifty-five thousand dollars, immediately took a train to New York City, put the money in a safe deposit box in a bank there, and enlisted in the army. After a four-year hitch the man went to New York to get his money—and on *that* day the bank teller from Syracuse was in New York on a vacation. He recognized the man who had robbed him four years before, followed him to the bank, and then notified a bank officer.

"They are much too expensive here," the librarian said severely. "In Oaxaca you can get four oranges for a *centavo!*"

Slocum sympathized with him. He returned the books he had been consulting and said goodbye. Next morning he had his kit from the Thieves' Market. He felt a slight regret for the real geologist, who by now was probably wondering why someone should steal so useless an object.

Slocum took the next train back to San Felipe.

10

There was no one else in the coach on the train going north. Slocum passed the time stringing necklaces on strong silk threads. He made emerald necklaces and ruby necklaces; he made a diamond and ruby necklace. Whey they were all done, he put them in a box. They were all jumbled together.

If anyone were to look at them at night, under the light of a kerosene lamp, the sudden view would be very impressive. The light would reflect from the myriad facets of the fake diamonds in a most convincing manner. And a greedy man, convinced that he was looking at Maximilian's treasure, would be prone to take the box of jewels at face value.

Late that afternoon he reached San Felipe. At the *fonda* he found a burro waiting for him. The burro was named Adelita. She had enormous brown eyes and a calm, amiable expression.

She tried her first trick when he was packing all his geological gear on her, together with all the camping equipment that an eager and not too experienced geologist would carry: a folding cot, a small tent, plenty of canned food, a coffee pot, a skillet, salt, bacon, and coffee. Everything looked battered, as if they had seen much use. They had; Slocum had bought most of it at the Thieves' Market.

He rented a good horse, with its saddle and gear. He bought a carbine and a Colt .44. Adelita waited patiently while he threw a diamond hitch on the load. She had blown out her stomach; when she decided that he had finished the hitch, she was going to let out her breath and the entire load would slide under her belly. This was a hoary old trick, and Slocum was ready. He waited till she had blown herself up as much as she could. Then he suddenly punched her in the belly. She let out a surprised *woof!* The air went out, she became her usual slim self, and he tightened the hitch immediately before she could take another deep breath. She laid one ear back while the other remained upright. This, as Slocum discovered, was what she did whenever she wanted to think things over.

She never tried that trick again. He had no doubt she would think up something else. He looked forward with amused interest to see what she would try next.

It happened immediately. Slocum set out, followed by Adelita at the end of a thirty-foot long reata. She balked right away and sat down in the dusty street. Slocum gave her rope a couple of round turns around his saddlehorn and then kicked his spurs into his horse's belly. After Adelita had skidded thirty-five feet across the rutted street, she changed her mind. She stood up and trotted obediently behind.

The country was covered with a wild jumble of mountains. Pine-clad on their upper slopes, the *mesquital*—mesquite, cactus, ocotillo—was lower down. Patches of good soil were crammed with growing corn and beans. Tiny, brilliant crimson splashes showed where chiles were growing in the dense green bushes. In the rivers Indian women, naked to the waist, scrubbed clothes on flat rocks. They giggled as the tall man with the hard face rode by.

It looked like a happy, prosperous land. On the surface.

Carrizo lay flat on his belly. The ground up on the ridge was covered with sharp stones. Every time he changed his position he grunted with pain. The muzzle of his carbine was pointed toward Adelita. He was not interested in the burro. She was grazing in a bored manner while Slocum, higher up the slope and partly concealed by a rocky outcrop, was holding his canteen to a trickle of ice-cold water that was dripping down the rocky face of the mountain. But he was standing at a poor angle for a shot to the heart.

So Carrizo waited. Unlike Slocum, he was impatient. He kept swinging the muzzle of his carbine from Slocum's leg to Adelita's head, then back again.

While Slocum waited for the canteen to fill, he looked down at Adelita. She laid her long ears back to show her disdain. Slocum laughed aloud. He enjoyed her company.

The canteen overflowed. Slocum screwed the cap on, walked down to his horse, hung the canteen by its strap over his horn, and turned to mount.

Carrizo fired. Like most people who were not accustomed to shooting downhill, he did not allow enough for the bullet's drop. It smashed Adelita's spine. She let out an agonized grunt and dropped like a stone. The echo of the shot bellowed in the narrow canyon. Slocum went flat with surprising speed and rolled over twice till he was behind a large boulder. With the reverberating echo it was impossible to be sure where the shot came from.

Carrizo cursed silently. Slocum was out of sight. The only thing to do now was to put him afoot and make pursuit impossible. With his second shot— Carrizo knew enough by now to aim higher—he killed Slocum's horse. He put two more bullets in the boulder behind which Slocum was waiting. Then he crawled backward till he was far enough downhill to stand up. He scrambled down to his horse, sweating in the heat and angry at his bad shooting. If the *gringo* had any sense, he would learn some hard facts from this experience and get the hell out of the mountains, go back to San Felipe, and stay there. He would give up looking for gold and silver and go back home.

If not, they would meet again. And next time, Carrizo swore, he would make sure to shoot in the horizontal plane. And to be much, much closer.

The second shot allowed Slocum to pinpoint its origin. He took a chance, waited till Carrizo had let off two more rounds, and then ran stooped to his dead horse. He jerked the carbine from its scabbard and went flat, this time behind the horse. There was no more firing.

Adelita was looking at him and braying. He saw right away that her spine was broken. She lifted her head and looked at him hopefully. He fired a shot into her brain. She shuddered and died. Slocum did not know how long the man up there was going to wait for him to expose himself. Whoever the man was, Slocum grimly promised himself, he would take care of him. He had liked Adelita.

He waited till dusk, wondering. Was it Robles? Was it one of his men? Was it someone else? When he could not see his hand held at arm's length, he left the shelter of the dead horse, circled around until he was on the reverse slope of the ridge where the shots had come from, and then began a slow, circuitous, infinitesimally slow approach.

And it was all for nothing. No one was there. He sat huddled for warmth, until sunrise. His teeth chattered with cold. Finally the sun rose. He quickly found the brass cartridge casings where the ejector had hurled them. The man, judging from the size of his footprints, had big feet. That *could* mean he was big. He had been waiting a long time: he had urinated twice. Therefore, Slocum reasoned, he had know that Slocum was coming; no one else would wait so long on the chance of an occasional wayfarer happening by. At the bottom of the slope Slocum examined the horse tracks. The horse's left front hoof had a deep nick on the outside.

The tracks led deeper into the mountains. Slocum definitely was not going in there on foot. There was only one thing to be done: return to San Felipe, get another horse and burro, and keep his eyes open. And move once again into the range. He cached Adelita's load and the saddle, saddle blanket, and bridle beside the trail. Then he turned back and started to hike the twenty miles to San Felipe.

During the afternoon a violent thunderstorm erupted. Lumps of hail the size of walnuts battered him; the heavy rain drenched him, and the scouring of the sheets of water sliding down the mountains washed away all the tracks. But not before he had found out that the man with the nicked horseshoe had not been following him, but had preceded him. It seemed, therefore, that this unknown person had just shot his burro and horse for amusement. Slocum couldn't figure it out.

After the rainstorm he had a hard five-hour walk to San Felipe in the hot sun. The sun dried his clothes. There was no other advantage to the day.

Slocum paid the livery stable owner for the dead animals.

"Malos hombres, malos hombres," the man muttered. Slocum wanted to rent another horse and burro, but Diaz said, "Ah, *señor,* suppose next time they not only kill my horse and burro, but kill you too? I shall have to sell you the horse and the burro. It is only logical, no? Also a saddle and bridle."

Slocum accepted. He said he would ride bareback to where he had cached the other saddle. He bought a *grullo* mare for fifty-five American dollars, and another burro for forty. The burro was named El Cigüeño—the stork—because of his thin legs. Slocum felt no affection for El Cigüeño, who plodded dully behind his horse. He had had no luck trying to find out who might have ridden the horse with the nicked shoe. The rain had washed out all the tracks that might have been left at San Felipe.

The cache was untouched. Seven gorged *zapilotes* waddled away from the half-stripped carcasses of Adelita and the horse. While Slocum saddled up and then adjusted the pack on El Cigüeño, they formed a half-circle and watched patiently with their cruel, indifferent eyes. Slocum thought it was no wonder *zapilotes* were so patient—everything came to them evenutally.

Slocum decided that his portrayal of an earnest geologist would not be convincing if he were to be seen effectively trailing a man who had shot at him. Geologists, when shot at, promptly abandon the area until things settle down.

So he rode slowly on. But because of the heavy rainstorm the day before, all tracks had been washed away. If he were to come across a track with a horseshoe with a nick in a left front shoe, he would take a deep interest in it. Otherwise, it was time to become a geologist.

Geologists always looked for things like discontinuities—places where one kind of rock overlay another kind. The boundary between the two formed an area of lesser resistance to lave flows welling up from the magma—the liquid rock that formed the earth's core. The lave carried within it the dissolved rare minerals—gold, silver, and so forth.

So whenever Slocum saw two different kinds of rock he dismounted and climbed, then chipped away with his hammer. Certain samples—nine times out of ten completely useless—he stowed away in small cloth bags. Then he drew a crude map showing exactly where the rock samples had come from. He took out a pocket compass and jotted down each sample's bearings.

It was the sort of thing that a conscientious geologist would do.

On the third day a lean, tough sixty-year-old named Oswaldo Gutierrez hunkered down under the shade of a clump of piñons and watched Slocum with deep interest. His calloused palms clung to the barrel of an old Springfield. The barrel was held to its splintered stock with baling wire.

Oswaldo's function was to roam the mountain above his tiny *milpas* at least once a day. If he saw anything that was not normal he had to report it to Robles immediately. Not reporting it would bring the most unpleasant consequences, as Robles had once pointed out to him as he sat his fine black horse in the middle of Oswaldo's tiny corn field.

Oswaldo saw the point of Robles's remark.

Now he judged that a man going around knocking off bits of rock from a mountain and stowing them in little sacks qualified as an unusual event. He followed Slocum's slow progress around the mountains. When dusk approached and Slocum prepared to make camp, Oswaldo turned and trotted on foot the twelve miles to Robles's headquarters. This was in the manager's wooden house at an abandoned silver mine. There was only one trail up to the mine, and people could be seen for miles as they approached.

Oswaldo was challenged three times in the last two miles. He was recognized each time and allowed to proceed.

"Well?" asked Robles. He tilted back an old kitchen chair against the wall.

Oswaldo began to describe the stranger and his unusual behavior.

The horse, Oswaldo said, was a six or seven-year-old *grullo*. Nothing special, he judged. The burro was somewhat thin. The man's clothes were old and worn. He carried a Colt and a carbine.

Robles had plenty of guns just then. Ammunition was what he needed, lots of it. If he killed the man and took the guns, it would be stupid, because the stranger was probably just an engineer of some kind. He was probably working for a rich *gringo* mining company. If he were killed, the *gringos* wouldn't like it. They would complain to Porfirio in Mexico City, and the president, who wanted to keep the big companies happy, would probably send a couple of companies of cavalry and maybe one or two mountain guns up into Robles's territory.

They would be afraid to leave the trails, but they would stir up the area, and make the *campesinos* even more resentful toward Robles. They might even find Robles's very comfortable headquarters and destroy it. And he had very little ammunition with which to resist them.

So, weighing everything in the balance, it would be best to keep the stranger under observation, yes. Kill him, no. Robles passed the word: Do not kill the *gringo*.

That evening Lucas Carrizo rode into the camp. He had a sort of pass, issued by Robles, which gave him the right to move anywhere he wanted without being molested. Since hardly anyone in Robles's group could read, the description was oral: *Dejen pasar un gordo, caballo negro, sin molestar.* Let the fat man on a black horse pass; do not bother him.

Carrizo shook hands with Robles, who cut short the formal greeting with the curt question, "Any ammunition?"

Carrizo unbuckled the saddlebags and dumped out the cartridges on the table. Robles grunted.

The arrangement was simple: Carrizo bought cattle from the small ranchers. They were afraid that Robles would rustle them anyway and kill them if they resisted. When Carrizo had assembled a herd of two to three hundred he had his *vaqueros* trail them to the northern cattle ranges. There they fetched good prices, since they had put on plenty of weight in the well-grassed valleys of their home ranges.

Carrizo then kept half of the proceeds. The other half went to Robles. This had to be done as secretly as possible in order to avoid any unpleasant reaction on the part of Porfirio Diaz, the president and dictator of Mexico. If he were to find out that Robles was benefiting from the relationship, Carrizo would suffer harsh treatment.

With his half of the proceeds Carrizo was forced by Robles to buy as many cartridges as he could in Durango. This town in Chihuahua was far enough away from Robles so that no one would make a connection between the two men. It was a mutually profitable arrangement. It had been going on for years. And neither man knew that the quiet man with the green eyes who had come to San Felipe was going to end it for both of them.

11

Finally some good luck came Slocum's way.

Diaz, the livery stable owner, had been told by the maid at the *fonda* about the rocks on the floor in little bags and the mysterious box. She had opened the box once and when she saw the small bottles of chemicals it contained she had thought Slocum was a *curandero*—a man who could cure sickness with herbs and potions.

She said this to Diaz, who explained to her patiently that the man was not a *curandero,* but someone who looked at rocks to see if they would tell him where gold was.

"A *brujo!*" she said triumphantly. "A witch!"

Diaz suddenly thought of something, cut her short, and entered his stable.

At one end he had built a lean-to out of scrap lumber and odd pieces of tin from flattened five-gallon cans. This slapdash structure housed his office, which consisted of a desk made from more scrap lumber. On top of the crudely carpentered desk was a box. This was where he kept his records, which consisted of jottings on odd scraps of paper. It was very secret, and all his help had been warned to stay away from the box. Since none of them could read, they obeyed without hesitation.

He opened the box and took out a rock the size of his fist. He had found it a month ago in a creekbed five miles north of San Felipe while he was out searching for a burro that had escaped from his stable. Diaz was fording the creek when he had seen the rock with its tiny golden glints stuck in the surface.

He picked it up. No one had noticed him. He stuck it promptly in his saddlebag and had been wondering what to do about it without starting a gold rush.

Now Diaz realized that he had someone in San Felipe who could answer his questions about the rock. He walked across the street to the *fonda*. The guests were sitting down for lunch. Diaz sat down next to Slocum and ordered a bottle of beer.

"How do you like the *grullo, señor?*" he began.

"A good horse."

Diaz cleared his throat. No one was listening. He bent over and said, "You are a *científico, señor?* This is what people say."

"I am a geologist."

"You know about rocks?"

Slocum nodded.

"*Señor*, I have a rock. I wish to know if it is valuable."

"Show it to me."

"It would not be wise to do it here," Diaz said, almost in a whisper.

"I understand. Where did you find this rock?" Slocum asked.

Diaz automatically lied. "Far from here," he said. He pointed diametrically opposite the creek. "Very far."

Then he added, raising his voice, "I have a chestnut gelding that might interest you."

"I would like to see it," Slocum said.

As they left Diaz said, "He can go all day like a locomotive. He never gets tired; the price is sensible."

"Perhaps we may come to an agreement," Slocum said.

They strolled to the stable, Diaz discoursing volubly on the wonder horse. Slocum nodded patiently. Once in the stable, Diaz abruptly stopped talking, took his rock from its hiding place, and handed it with suppressed excitement to Slocum, who immediately saw it was a worthless chunk of iron pyrites, a metallic-looking sulphide.

It was then that Slocum saw his chance: here was a man who was dreaming of millions to be extracted from the gold mine he had discovered; he was encouraged in this vision by a man whom he respected as an expert geologist; and, when the bubble would burst, Slocum would have a full-time, energetic public detractor who would tell everyone he came across that *whatever* the *gringo* was, he was no geologist.

Slocum scraped the rock with his thumbnail. He frowned. He lifted the rock to his mouth and ran his tongue lightly over the surface as if he were tasting it. The gestures meant nothing: they were designed to impress someone who knew nothing.

Diaz bit his lip as he waited. Slocum finally lifted his head and said quietly, "Gold." Diaz's face broke out into a delighted smile. Slocum hefted the rock in his palm. He said judiciously, "It should assay twenty, twenty-five thousand American dollars to the ton."

Diaz's mouth opened in delirious astonishment. Then he said, in an attempt to show he was a businessman, "Assay?" He had never heard the word before.

"Yes," Slocum said. "To make absolutely sure about the percentage of gold in this ore sample. They will analyze it scientifically and then write it down on a piece of paper. This paper is important; it proves you have found a valuable gold mine."

"Do I have to tell them where the gold came from?"

"No. You take the assay report and show it to people. Then they will invest in your mine so that you will be able to buy equipment and hire workers."

"Is this all there is to it?"

It was not all, but Slocum did not want to make Diaz's eventual disappointment harder than it had to be.

"Yes. First things first, however. The nearest assay office is in Guadalajara."

"That is far away!" Diaz said with dismay.

Slocum shrugged.

"Pardon, *señor*. What then?"

"Go there immediately. Get your assay done. Then file your claim for the mine before anyone else does."

"Yes, yes! How much do I owe you, *señor*?"

"Nothing, my friend. *Vaya con Dios*."

Diaz grabbed his hand warmly and shook it. *"Muchas gracias, señor! Muchas gracias!"*

"Por nada," Slocum said. "It is nothing." And, indeed, Slocum thought, that was literally true. He added, "There is something you can do for me, if you wish."

"Yours to command," Diaz said. He was busy saddling one of his better horses.

"There is a man who may come into your stable." Diaz also did horse-shoeing, Slocum had observed. "He rides a horse with a nick in its left front shoe. I want to know who he is."

"On which side of the shoe is the nick?"

"Outside."

Diaz slid the bridle over the horse's head. He nodded. He kept his face calm. He knew the horseshoe in question. It belonged on Carrizo's fine black horse. He himself had nailed it in place. He would have liked to return Slocum's favor, but first he would have to find out the *gringo's* intention. Carrizo was a wealthy and unpleasant man. Then Diaz suddenly remembered how Slocum had humiliated Carrizo for insulting the young priest. The maid at the *fonda* had breathlessly told him the whole story while they were making love on a sweaty horse blanket in the back of the stable.

And Diaz immediately guessed the rest of the story: Carrizo had to be the sniper who had tried to kill Slocum, but had killed the *gringo's* rented horse and his burro. When Diaz looked at the affair on a purely economic basis, Carrizo had, in effect, acted as Diaz's agent in the profitable sale of another burro and horse to Slocum.

One could not repay that with dangerous information.

Moreover, if Carrizo ever found out that Diaz had told Slocum about the nicked shoe, he was perfectly capable of killing Diaz. And what *alguacil*—if this should occur—would dare arrest a man who was an honored associate of Alejandro Robles?

"Certainly, *señor*. I will let you know."

He mounted.

"To Guadalajara?" Slocum asked.

"If I ride hard all night I will be in Guadalajara in the morning. *Hasta la vista, señor!*"

Slocum lifted a hand in farewell as Diaz rode away at a fast trot. Next time they met Diaz would not be friendly at all.

That evening Slocum waited till dusk. Then he rode out of San Felipe. This attracted attention for two reasons: first, because it was contrary to his usual pattern of movements; second, hardly anyone left on a trip in the evening. Bandits in the mountains made such travelling too risky.

Two hours later and eight miles east of San Felipe he halted. Halfway up a steep slope covered with scrub piñon, on one of his earlier trips, he had noticed a cave opening. Caves were not unusual in this part of the Sierra, but he had filed this one away for future reference. Now the time had come to make use of it.

He rode up to the cave. He dismounted, spread his map flat on the ground, and weighed each corner down with a small stone. He took a candle from his saddlebag and lit it. He hunkered down above the map and pretended to study it. With the index finger of his left hand he traced a meaningless line across the map.

He did this for ten minutes. Candlelight could be seen for amazing distances on a dark night.

If riding out in the evening, and looking at a map by candlelight halfway up a mountain wouldn't attract Robles's unsavory attention quickly, Slocum told himself, he'd eat the damn map.

And for the second time in one day Slocum was lucky. Oswaldo Gutierrez, going out of his hut to chase away some coatimundis which were raiding his corn fields, saw the candlelight. No one he knew would be doing such a thing; too many evil things, including *brujas*—witches—were abroad at night.

Oswaldo was not as superstitious as the other *campesinos*. He ran down the slope at a diagonal. He knew every foot of the mountain. He did not trip or make any noise except for the slap of his *huaraches* on the hard, rocky soil.

He was in time to see Slocum trace a line on the map with his forefinger. Oswaldo watched as Slocum folded the map, produced his pocket compass, looked at it, and then, after blowing out the candle, mounted. Then he rode slowly up the slope toward the cave.

Oswaldo sat down on a big rock and watched with fascination. He knew about the cave. Everyone did. It was just a cave, like all the other caves. Bats lived in it and flew out in clouds at dusk and hunted all night. Oswaldo shuddered. They were vampire bats and he knew terrible stories about them. And they also carried the sickness that made people thirsty and bark like a dog.

Oswaldo could not understand why the man—now he recognized him as the one he had seen earlier—should look at the paper and then go into a cave full of bats. Maybe he was a *brujo* looking to consult the King of the Bats? Such things had happened. He shuddered. Or maybe the man was mad? He waited.

• • •

Slocum lit the candle and, holding it aloft, entered the cave. He was careful: there were openings in the floor of some caves which went straight down for hundreds of feet; some of them, indeed, had no bottom that anyone had been able to discover. The floor of the cave was covered with a deep layer of guano dropped by untold generations of bats. Some baby bats clung to the ceiling upside down; their red eyes glared at him. But corpses and skeletons littered the floor. He cleared a space on the floor and leaned back against the wall. The guano had a sharp, not unpleasant odor. He sat there for two hours and thought about Robles. It had been months since Wesley Putnam had been murdered. Slocum still felt the same cold rage whenever he thought about it. He had done everything he could think of to force Robles to approach him. He could only hope that the approach would be made in such a way that left Slocum a chink through which he could escape—and the chink would be Robles's overpowering greed at the thought of being the man who would seize the fabulous treasure of Maximilian, an amount which would ensure his wealth for the rest of his life.

It would be something which he would not like to entrust to any of his henchmen.

It would bring Robles out of the Sierra in person.

After two hours—enough time to convince anyone who might be watching that he was in the cave for something more interesting than bat guano, which was used for a high-potency fertilizer—Slocum left the cave.

He took the saddlebags from his horse, and went

back into the cave. He filled both bags with rocks. Oswaldo watched patiently. Slocum came out with the filled saddlebags, draped them across the saddle, then rode downhill and back to San Felipe.

The whole thing was too mysterious and inexplicable for Oswaldo. He had no doubt that Robles would have to be told. He sighed and began his long hike to Robles's headquarters.

"The *gringo* came to the cave at night?"

"*Sí.*" Oswaldo deferentially removed his sombrero.

"He looked at a paper first?"

"*Sí, jefe.*"

"Then?"

"He went went into the cave. He stayed there the time it takes the Road of the Ghosts to turn this part of a circle." Oswaldo held his thumb and forefinger three inches apart. Thus he indicated the movement made by the Milky Way while Slocum was inside. Oswaldo had never seen a watch and would never know how to tell time, even if he had one. But his sense of the passage of time was amazingly accurate.

"Two hours," Robles said impatiently. "Then?"

"Then he came out, took his saddlebags, and went into the cave again. When he came out the saddlebags were filled. He rode away to San Felipe."

"Of what use is bat shit to a *gringo*?"

"None, *mi jefe*. But it makes good fertilizer."

Gracias, Oswaldo." Robles took out a silver peso and tossed it to Oswaldo, who protested it was not necessary.

Robles waved him away. He thought that this cave business was very interesting. If there was some sort of a business about to be conducted there, he wanted a cut of the proceeds. But why at night? And the piece of paper was clearly a map. But no one needed a map to know that bat guano was in caves. Puzzling, the whole thing!

Oswaldo had not moved. He kept turning his cheap straw sombrero around and around by the brim.

"Not enough?" Robles demanded.

"Sí, sí, jefe! Bastante! I have thought of something which may be stupid. But then, I am a man without education."

"Be quick, then."

"When I was much younger, people said that they had seen many loaded burros pass by, with many soldiers and a captain, going toward this mountain. A day later the captain was seen riding back alone. The burros were wandering around without packs. They were to be had for the taking. But they were branded with the army's brand; no one dared to touch. Eventually the *tigres* killed them all."

"Well?"

"The soldiers came from the direction of Queretaro, *mi jefe*."

Robles was not well versed in Mexican history. "Why do you waste my time with your peasant stories?" he demanded.

Oswaldo had never gone to school. But he had listened to his elders carefully. "Queretaro," he said patiently, "is where they shot the Emperor Maximilian."

"So?"

"His treasure—diamonds, emeralds, gold—was with him before he was shot. Then it was never found."

"Ah," Robles said slowly. "Ah."

Slocum dropped the rocks from the saddlebags in the darkness. He slung the bags over his shoulder and dismounted in the small corral kept at the *fonda* for the convenience of horsemen who were staying there. Once inside his room, he sprawled out on his cot. He was exhausted. After he had dozed for an hour, arms outspread, he got up. He took off his shirt. From his money belt he extracted the ten old Mexican gold coins for which he had exchanged some of his double eagles in Mexico City. These he dropped into one of the saddlebags. Then he dropped in five necklaces and a handful of the glass emeralds and rubies. He closed the flap and then opened it for a quick look.

"By God," he said quietly. Even the knowledge that everything in it was fake except the gold coins made his heart pound faster. It looked very impressive. He buckled the flap shut. Then he leaned back on the cot and went back to sleep.

Now there was nothing to do but wait. He had baited the trap well. Somewhere out there, he hoped, there was a greedy bear lifting its cruel head as it sniffed the honey.

12

"It is worth nothing," the man in the assay office said. People always brought in iron pyrites with great hopes. He set down the specimen Diaz had brought with him. Diaz grabbed it from the scarred, splintered wooden counter and said, "I want to speak to your superior." He spoke as calmly as he could, even though he was furious. He had ridden all night and had not slept or eaten.

"Why, *señor*?"

"Why? Because, my friend, you are incompetent."

"And, *señor*, I ask you once more why you wish to speak to my superior?"

"Because you clearly do not know gold when you

see it. Since this is gold ore of high purity and value, your inability to observe this shows that you lack qualifications for your position here. With your permission, *señor*."

The clerk sighed. This was a very common reaction with the people who brought in iron pyrites. He shrugged wearily. He went away to the far end of the room. He came back with a thin, cadaverous man with a mournful face. He wore a cap with a visor of cracked green celluloid.

"Yes?"

"Your assistant is incompetent!"

The man sighed. "On the contrary, *señor*," he said patiently.

Diaz slammed the rock on the counter. "He claimed that this is *not* gold! he shouted. "Doesn't that make him incompetent?"

The man picked it up and looked at the bright specks. Then he replaced it gently on the counter. Angry prospectors had slammed down enough rocks in his tenure to ruin the surface, and he was not going to make it worse.

"It is iron pyrites," he said gently.

"It is *gold!* I know it is gold! A geologist tested it properly! And neither of you has tested it!"

"How did he test it?" the man asked softly.

"He tested it for weight like this!" Diaz snatched the rock and hefted it the way he had seen Slocum do it.

"And then he licked it, like this!" Diaz brought the rock to his mouth and licked it. The two assayers smiled. Diaz said, "Are you making fun of me?"

"No, *señor*," the older man said. "Whoever the man is, he is not a geologist. The test for gold is very simple. One does not lift the ore; one does not lick it. We do not see gold here. We see iron pyrites. You can read, *señor?*"

"Of course!"

"Very well." He turned to the younger man and jerked his head at a bookshelf across the room. In a moment the man was back with a thick volume. He opened to the heading marked *"Oro.* Gold." He lifted the book so that Diaz could see the book's title: *Mineral Analysis.* Then he spun the book around so that the text faced the fuming Diaz. His forefinger pointed to a passage.

Diaz read: "The most malleable of metals. One ounce of gold can be beaten so that it covers one square acre." The man took out a jackknife and pried out one of the glints that had so fascinated Diaz when he saw the rock at the bottom of Cañada La Cruz.

He put it on a metal plate and then struck it with a hammer. It crunched to powder under the blow.

"You see? Not gold. Gold would flatten out."

He put the hammer down and turned the pages of the book until he came to the heading "Iron Pyrites." He found the passage he was looking for. He turned the book so that it faced Diaz and indicated where Diaz should read.

"Iron pyrites is a sulphide of iron. Sulphur will be released by the application of an open flame. There will be a strong odor of sulphur."

"Have you read it?"

"Yes," Diaz said in a sullen whisper.

The assayer lit a match and held it to the crushed particle of iron pyrites. A strong smell of sulphur filled the air.

"I see," Diaz said slowly.

"I am afraid that this person has been amusing himself at your expense, my friend. Whoever he is, he is not a geologist."

Diaz was almost in tears.

Diaz rode back to San Felipe. He arrived at nine at night. He handed the reins to the stable boy, did not respond to that person's greeting. He strode furiously to the *fonda* where the false geologist was staying.

The guests were just sitting down for supper. Bowls of beans and rice were on the table. A platter of broiled turkey legs was being carried in by the maid as Diaz entered the patio. She blushed. Diaz never came to the *fonda*. She thought he had come in order to ask her to come to the stable later and make love.

Instead he paid no attention to her. He walked straight to the table where Slocum was sitting. Diaz stopped across the table from Slocum, leaned on it, and, resting his knuckles on the edge for balance, opened his mouth. His face was red with anger. Slocum looked at him with an expression of mild interest, although he knew very well the reason for the man's rage. Carrizo was seated at the far end of the table. He had just scooped some beans onto a tortilla and had paused to listen.

"You call yourself a geologist!" Diaz shouted. "You—"

The maid tugged at his sleeve. She had seen what Slocum had done to Carrizo. She was afraid that Diaz would be forced to undergo the same process. Slocum noticed her terrified, beseeching look. He immediately understood the connection between Diaz and the woman.

"One moment," Slocum said, holding up his hand

to stop the incoherent flow of words. "You have been to the assayer?"

"*Sí!* And—"

"And he told you that the specimen was worth nothing, I suppose?"

Diaz looked at Slocum more closely now. He was shaken by the calm, smiling face and the air of assurance.

"Of course! He said—"

Slocum said patiently, "One moment, *señor*. Did you tell him where you found it?"

"No!"

"Are you sure? Not even the general area?"

That was something that Diaz now remembered he had done in his rage. He had told the assayer that the rock had come from Cañada La Cruz.

"I think maybe I did," Diaz said slowly. His rage had dissipated.

"You see?" Slocum said gently. "He tells you it is worth nothing. Then he finds out where it comes from, because he has cleverly persuaded you that there is no point in keeping it a secret any more."

A man like Diaz, Slocum knew, would be suspicious of everyone's motives.

Diaz swallowed this completely imaginary explanation like parched soil takes in a sudden rain.

"Assayers are known for this unpleasant habit," Slocum went on.

"Yes, but—"

"Did he remove the rock from your presence at any time?"

Diaz said slowly, "I think he took it into the back room to show to the other man. I am not sure, I was so excited. Maybe he did that. Then I was so disturbed that I did not notice much."

Slocum sighed. "He took the rock in back; he then picked up a piece of iron pyrites—"

"What?"

"Iron pyrites. It is a mixture of sulphur with other substances. He brought out this iron pyrites specimen. People are always bringing in iron pyrites thinking they have found gold. Did he make the hammer test?"

"Yes, he did that." Diaz's anger had ebbed away completely.

"And did he burn a piece to make the sulphur smell?"

"Yes," Diaz said grudgingly.

"You were convinced by that, of course. Then you believed everything he said."

Diaz nodded. He could not think of anything to say. Slocum's questions showed that he knew what he was talking about. And the fact that the assayers had laughed at him made Diaz positive that they had laughed because they had successfully switched specimens.

"But why would they do that?" Diaz demanded, almost in tears.

"Because they work with someone who is doubtless up in the mountains looking at the place where you found your rock; when they locate it they will establish a claim."

Diaz's rage flowered again. He cursed silently for a long time. Then he spun around and walked out of the *fonda*. That night he blackened both eyes of the maid after they had made love. She wept silently.

• • •

"He is very clever," Carrizo said. He tapped his forehead. They were sitting on the veranda of Robles's headquarters. Far below wiggled the silver thread of the Rio Cienaga.

"But no geologist?"

"Absolutely not."

"Why are you so sure?" Robles had confidence in Carrizo's shrewd instincts.

Carrizo shrugged. "In the Sierra over many years I have met many engineers, many geologists. Most of them were *gringos*. None of them spoke good Spanish. This one speaks Spanish like you and I. None of them would have been so calm if accused publicly the way this fool Diaz attacked him. He just sat there with a little smile and listened."

Robles brooded over Carrizo's remarks. The *gringo* had gone into the cave at night, hardly a geologist's way of investigation. It was also Carrizo's careful opinion that the man was a fraud. It was time to ride into San Felipe for a confrontation.

He slapped his thigh. *"Bien!"* He turned and yelled, "Tomás! Henrique! Pablito! Jorge! Alberto! We ride tonight into San Felipe!"

Carrizo said, "Do you have any cattle for me?"

Robles stood up and stretched, with his gaze fixed on the misty blue ranges of the Sierra.

"Lucas, when I am finished with this *gringo*, there will be no more cattle, and no more buying ammunition by the saddlebag."

Carrizo looked at him without comprehension. Robles laughed and went inside to buckle on his gunbelt.

• • •

At nine that night Slocum was lying on his cot with his arms hanging down. A candle was burning on the small, battered table beside the cot. On it were a few Mexican coins. The thin door was held shut with a small hook and eye screwed into the jamb. The saddlebags were in a corner. His gunbelt hung over the doorknob.

Without warning the door burst open. Someone had kicked it in. At the same time, the wooden shutters covering the window openings were shattered by a carbine butt.

Slocum felt a kind of relief. Robles had come at last!

When he looked up, four carbine barrels were pointed at him through the shattered shutters. In the doorway stood a tall man with a big sombrero. He had a hard, brooding face with a tight smile. He was holding a Colt .45 in his right hand. It was pointing negligently at the floor in a way that suggested that he was in complete control of the situation.

"I am Robles," he said. "Sit up."

Slocum felt a fierce exultation. The last act of the play was about to begin.

A man in back of Robles removed Slocum's gunbelt from the door and buckled it on. The man was now wearing two gunbelts. Ordinarily this might have been an amusing sight, but somehow the man looked too hard-bitten.

Slocum sat up. Robles toured the room, inspecting it. Slocum looked at the man who was wearing his own gun plus Slocum's. This was Jorge Armendariz, a man who had murdered the rent collector of the hacienda where he grew up, and later killed the two deputy sheriffs who had been sent to arrest him.

Armendariz moved swiftly to the cot. He reached underneath it and removed Slocum's carbine. He held it in the crook of his left arm.

"Very good," Robles said. He had not noticed it.

"Can I keep it?" Armendariz asked.

"Yes." Both men stank of horse sweat. They had obviously ridden hard for several hours. Robles's boot kicked gently at the saddlebags.

"You interest me, *señor*," Robles said suddenly. It was the voice of a man used to command. Armendariz had small black eyes and a steady stare. Slocum judged him to be a killer.

"Why?" All that mattered was to keep the game going until he had boxed Robles in such a way that he could kill him and escape.

Robles grinned. "A geologist who knows nothing about minerals? A man who visits caves at night?"

It was time to test Robles's reactions. Slocum's hand suddenly shot out toward the little bedside table. Robles's arm came up. The gun pointed at Slocum's heart. Armendariz jacked a cartridge into the carbine's chamber. Good reaction times, Slocum thought. Fast, precise movements. These were dangerous men.

"Please be careful," Robles said. "If we had been stupid men, you would be dead now."

"With all these strangers in my room," Slocum said, "I was afraid someone might help himself to my loose change." He scooped up the coins and dropped them into his pocket. Armendariz's eyes glittered at the implied insult. Robles smiled.

"*Señor*," he said abruptly, "to business. What do you have in those saddlebags?"

"Nothing of interest."

"Just tell me, *señor*."

"Oh, socks, a spare shirt, a razor, soap. Things like that."

Robles hooked the saddlebags with his pointed boot toe and pulled them close to him. "Nothing more?"

"Needle and thread. Oh, yes, a small bottle of iodine. And a pair of gloves."

"I see." Robles suddenly picked up the saddlebag, unbuckled it, and tilted it toward the candlelight.

The light was caught by the facets on the glass diamonds. It was refracted and broken into flashes of rainbow colors. The rubies glowed like ripe cherries. The emeralds shone like limes. The old gold coins provided a rich backdrop.

"Jesús y María!" Robles swore.

Armendariz's face showed no expression, but his eyes widened.

Robles ran his hand through the jewels. The rate of his breathing increased. He reached inside, hung three necklaces on his fingers, and held them high. The candlelight made them look magnificent. Even Slocum was impressed.

Robles let the necklaces slip off his fingers till they collapsed on the others still in the saddle bag. He next reached in, rummaged around the bottom, and hauled out a handful of the gold coins. Slocum had relied on their authenticity to vouch for the rest of the fakes in the bag.

Robles hefted the gold. He began to breathe faster, as if the heavy weight of the gold were sensuous fingers caressing him. Then he managed to control himself. The naked lust in his eyes went away. In its place came a look so cold and menacing and emotionless that it reminded Slocum of a rattlesnake about to strike.

"From the cave?" Robles asked.

"What cave?"

With a lightning-fast movement, Robles smashed his Colt barrel against Slocum's left cheek. Slocum saw it coming and jerked his head to the right. His head rode with the blow, so he only received a cut that was a quarter of an inch deep instead of the whole cheek being ripped in two.

"Very fast," Robles said approvingly. He jerked his head at Slocum. Past experience had told Armendariz what to do. He pointed the carbine at Slocum's belly while Robles bent down, grabbed Slocum's hair with his left hand so that Slocum would not be able to move. This time the blow with the Colt cut to the bone.

"Ah," Robles said, satisfied. Blood slid down from the long gash. "From the cave?"

Slocum shook his head. He bore no resentment for the blow. He had done similar things in his life in order to secure information that could be achieved no other way.

Robles nodded understandingly. The two blows would have persuaded most men. The fact that Slocum was silent was not unexpected. Robles knew that the *gringo* would eventually talk. There were a whole series of tricks at his disposal. The Apache glove, the Yaqui thing with the testicles, the greased, sharpened stake up the rectum, among others. But it would be best to begin with the minor ones, and work his way gradually up the scale. It was always interesting to see just where a man would break.

He walked briskly to the smashed shutters and yelled out into the street, "Oswaldo."

"*Sí, jefe!*"

"Come inside."

"*Sí, jefe!*"

"Henrique."

"*Sí.*"

"You also."

Oswaldo and Henrique entered and waited. Henrique was tall and wiry, with the calloused, powerful arms of a man who had been a *campesino* from birth. A machete stroke had left a scar that ran vertically from his hairline to the bottom of his jaw. The machete had removed his left eye and left a red socket behind.

Robles nodded at Slocum. Henrique pulled him erect and methodically tied his wrists behind his back with a length of rawhide.

"*Agua,*" Robles said. There was a pitcher of water standing in a corner. Henrique picked it up and poured the water slowly over the rawhide. As it dried it would constrict till it would be buried deep in the flesh. Little things like that always weakened a man's resolve not to talk.

Robles said, "Oswaldo. Do you know this man?"

"*Sí.* He is the man who went into the cave."

Robles looked at Slocum. Slocum slowly shook his head. Robles nodded. They pulled him to his feet and took him through the patio while the frightened guests watched. Slocum's horse had been saddled. Slocum was hoisted into the saddle. No one said a word. The group rode silently out of San Felipe.

Robles decided to spend the night in Oswaldo's shack. He would search the cave as soon as it was light. The *campesino*, his wife, and their three children took their ragged blankets and filed outside. Fifty feet from

Oswaldo's house a tall oak grew. A nod at the tree and then at Slocum told Armendariz what to do. Without a word he unhooked his reata. A stiff-armed push against the mounted prisoner was enough to topple him heavily to the ground. His left boot caught in the stirrup.

His horse, rendered jittery by the sudden unaccustomed weight on one side, danced nervously in a tight circle. It bent its neck to stare at its master. Slocum, with his wrists behind his back, was helpless. As the horse revolved, the movement forced dirt into Slocum's wound.

Robles watched and grinned. The worse treatment the average prisoner received in the beginning, the faster he tended to talk later on. Now the *gringo* would have a night filled with pain and discomfort while he thought about what the day might bring. Such musings usually produced excellent results.

Armendariz unhooked Slocum's boot from the stirrup. He dragged him by one ankle till he had positioned him under the tree to his satisfaction. He tied one end of the reata to the taut rawhide binding his wrists. He threw the other end of the reata over a low branch of the oak. Then he hoisted away.

Slocum's arms went up behind him. The cruel pressure of the lift forced him to his knees and then to his feet as Armendariz kept hauling away.

Armendariz kept pulling vigorously. When Slocum was on tiptoe, his arms went straight up, his head and shoulders were forced over as if he were in a deep bow. Satisfied at last, Armendariz made the end of the reata fast to a low branch and stepped back while he waited for Robles's approval.

The pressure against Slocum's shoulder joints was

agonizing. In spite of the night chill at the high altitude, he began to sweat. Perspiration beaded his forehead.

Robles came out of the hut. He was eating one of the tortillas that had been prepared by Oswaldo's wife for her family. The rest of the food would be consumed by Robles's men.

"How are you feeling, my friend?" he asked genially.

Slocum lifted his head. Because of the darkness Robles could not see his eyes. If he had, one sight of the cold, remorseless stare, totally without fear or apprehension, waiting only for the correct moment to kill, would have made him kill Slocum immediately.

He stepped forward and slapped Slocum between his shoulder blades. The impact against the cruelly strained joints felt as if barbed wire was being dragged through the tendons and muscles. Sweat formed and dripped down his back.

"Pass a pleasant night, my friend," Robles said. "Tomorrow we will talk some more. Perhaps your memory will improve."

After he had left, Armendariz and three others sat in a semicircle around Slocum and watched him the rest of the night. They warmed themselves from a fire made of dried oak branches, but far enough away so that Slocum could not benefit from the heat. Once during the night Slocum looked up. Henrique's face was lit from his blind side. His empty eye socket glowed in the fire like the eye of a wolf coming close to a camp at night. Slocum let his head fall again. His cheek began to throb painfully, the first sign of infection.

13

It was the worst night Slocum had ever passed. His cheek throbbed. He was sure it was infected by being shoved into the dirt. It was hard for him to pump air into his lungs, since his position thrust his shoulders and ribs into such a cramped position that they did not permit the lungs their normal expansion.

The pain felt as if a row of blowtorches were focused deep inside his back at the junction of his upper arms with the shoulder blades.

Two of the men slept. Once Robles came by on a silent tour of inspection. But Armendariz had heard him coming and prodded them awake. Robles grabbed Slocum's chin between his thumb and first two fingers and squeezed hard. He was angry because Slocum still had not talked about the whereabouts of the rest of the treasure. Then he walked to Oswaldo's hut. Oswaldo's family had withdrawn far up the mountain. His wife wanted to avoid a likely rape.

Armendariz suddenly let the reata slide down. It was morning. Slocum pitched forward on his face, driving still more dirt into his face wound. The agonizing strain on his back had disappeared. His shoulder joints still ached, but at least the terrible strain had stopped. At last he could breathe freely. His lungs sucked in deep drafts of air. This gave him such pleasure that he was smiling when Robles appeared. It gave Robles pause. Mexicans were a hardy people, inured to pain and death, but this *gringo* was of a different order entirely. Robles began to have serious doubts that his regimen of torture would work.

So Robles mused while he gazed downward. Slocum returned his look with a stare of such cold, confident hatred that it was like a challenging slap in the face.

It seemed that the *gringo* would not be talking as quickly as Robles had expected. Nor did he have a family to threaten—the technique which kept Oswaldo and so many others in the Sierra in line. So Robles decided he would simply increase the intensity of the pain when he worked on Slocum again. As he walked back to eat a quick breakfast of eggs and tortillas, he brooded over which should be the next torture: The Apache glove? The Yaqui one with the testicles? The greased, sharpened stake up the rectum?

• • •

They pushed Slocum flat against the ground while Robles held up the kerosene lamp he had taken from Oswaldo's hut.

"Where is the rest?"

"Rest of what?"

Slocum's face was pressed hard against the ground. He had not slept all night. His cheek throbbed and his back seemed to be on fire.

Robles suddenly kicked him with his pointed boot. Slocum's head snapped to one side with the impact. The scab that had formed during the night broke open. Blood dripped onto the ground; Some oozed into his mouth.

Slocum wasted no time hating. He went over his problem: how to get Robles alone. He spat out blood. Slocum had solved that problem with Duran, but he had had a sort of a friendly relationship with Duran. With Robles he had nothing except the man's passion to get hold of Maximilian's treasure. And then the thought came that he had not planned this one carefully enough; he had left too much to chance.

And Robles did not look like the kind of man who made mistakes. Had Slocum underestimated Robles? It was beginning to look that way.

"*Gringo!*"

Slocum turned his head sideways and looked up at Robles, who was standing beside him with his thumbs hooked into his cartridge belt.

"Cold last night, no?"

Slocum said nothing.

"It *was* cold, *amigo*. Your hands were cold. So I think I will make you a pair of gloves."

Armendariz began to smile.

"See? Jorge knows how warm the gloves will make you."

Armendariz's smile broadened. Robles turned to Armendariz and nodded. Slocum knew what they were talking about. He braced himself. Armendariz pulled out his knife. On it the maker had etched the three words *"Mato sin piedad,* I kill without pity." Robles let out a sharp whistle. Two more men arrived. They knew what was wanted. They held Slocum's right arm rigid. Armendariz approached.

Slocum knew what was going to happen. He had come across men and women left by Apaches on the wagon trail running east to west across Apache Pass. The first step in the torture process was called the Apache glove. This was not fatal—that was why it was the first step—but it was agonizing enough.

A circular incision was made with a sharp knife all the way around the arm just below the elbow. Then the skin was slowly peeled away from the raw flesh underneath. If the man who did it was skillful and patient, he could peel the entire skin from the arm till it looked like a red glove turned inside out.

"You seem to know about the glove," Robles said. Slocum's eyes flicked upwards. He had noticed a *zapilote* far overhead. Those foul-smelling birds angered him. Robles followed his glance. Then he smiled. Slocum's flicker of annoyance had given Robles an excellent idea—if the glove did not work.

Armendariz kept his prized knife razor-sharp. With the point, he quickly and accurately traced a circle completely around Slocum's upper arm just below the elbow. Only the skin was sliced open. Tiny red beads welled up on the circle; it looked like a ruby necklace made for a doll. Armendariz wiped his knife on his pants. Then he sheathed it. His dirty fingernails dug at the loosened skin. Slocum clenched his teeth to prevent himself from crying out. He felt he could handle the pain. Robles saw the confidence in Slocum's face. And once more Robles noticed the distaste in Slocum's eyes as he saw more *zapilotes* joining the first one. They had learned that when several men clustered about a man who was on the ground, there would be dead meat for them soon. And now the birds had drifted somewhat lower.

Robles suddenly said, "Stop." He had a better idea.

Armendariz halted his work. He turned his puzzled expression toward Robles.

"Jorge. Saddle up. I have an errand. You know the mixture of plants the *indios* use? The one they call *yaa-askidi?*"

"*Sí.*"

This concoction was known to the Aztecs. Their priests used it to induce visions. It had the peculiar property of completely paralyzing the voluntary muscle system while it did not affect the involuntary muscles. Thus, a man would be completely inert, unable to move a muscle, while his breathing and heart continued as before. The mind was not affected. The Aztecs believed that a man, apparently dead, and not responding to any stimulus, was in fact dead, and so able to contact the souls of the dead and tell them what was happening to their loved ones still alive.

"Who would have some?"

"A *bruja* named Antonita, far up Arroyo Madera Colorada."

Robles gave him two silver pesos. "Enough?"

"*Sí.*"

"Bring it to the mine headquarters. Henrique!"

"*Sí.*"

"Get Tomás to help you. Take the *gringo* and spread-eagle him on the rocky flat back of the mine shaft. Strip him naked first, and bring the clothes to my house."

Henrique gave him a puzzled look.

"After I'm finished this time," Robles said, "he'll want to get dressed and help us all he can. *Entendido?*"

Henrique didn't get it, but he was willing to trust Robles. One thing was sure—it was bound to be much more imaginative than the Apache glove. A slow smile spread across his face. Robles was very clever with ways of making men talk.

By the time Armendariz had returned with the *yaa-askidi,* Slocum had been brought to the mine headquarters. He had been stripped naked and then spread-eagled on the rocky flat where Robles had told the men to stake him. The reason for this was because the sun's heat, reflected from the heated rock, created strong upward-welling thermals on which the *zapilotes* liked to coast while their extraordinary vision sought out the land below for dead or dying creatures.

Stakes had been driven deep at the ends of his outstretched arms and legs. Rawhide thongs lashed each wrist and ankle tightly to its stake. Movement was impossible. Henrique had done this many times before, and he was an expert at it.

Next, following Robles's orders, he cut himself an oak branch six feet long and two inches in diameter. He put a razor-sharp point on it with his knife. Then he dug a hole with a rusty shovel that was kept inside a little shed next to the corral, where oats and odd bits of harness were stored.

When the hole was six feet deep he stopped. He placed the stake upright in it, with the sharp end upward, and then he smeared some old grease from the abandoned hoisting machinery over the point. Next he stamped the loosened soil firmly around the bottom of the stake. It could now hold plenty of weight, Slocum knew—for instance, his hundred and ninety pounds.

Next Henrique took a bucket of water and poured it over the rawhide bonds. When they would dry, no movement at all would be possible. Then the men waited for Robles to appear. The sun flared in the sky. The rawhide began to dig in as the water evaporated. High up in the brilliant blue sky the *zapilotes* saw the old pattern once more: men around another one lying on his back. They began to circle.

The sun hurt Slocum's eyes. He turned his head aside. On the rocky flat where he had been staked out there were large gray masses of stones which had not yet been eroded down to the same grade where he lay. Robles stepped from behind one of the stones. He had been studying Slocum's reaction to the *zapilotes*. He was delighted.

In his hand he carried a cup of water. Small round leaves were floating in it. They were a pale olive green.

"You are thirsty?" He held the cup to Slocum's lips while Slocum drank it greedily. He paid no attention to the leaves; he thought it was just typical Mexican casualness. The water was delicious nevertheless. Robles smiled down at him. Slocum wanted to drink quarts more of the water, but it was clear that there wouldn't be any.

The sun was beginning to burn his naked body; blisters were starting to pop up on his stomach and shoulders.

The drug took effect with startling suddenness. Slocum did not realize what was happening until he tried to blink away the sweat that was trickling into his eyes. His eyelids refused to close. This worried him. Next he tried to move his fingers in order to encourage circulation through the tightly constricted arteries. The fingers did not move. He tried to move his head from left to right. Nothing. He began to feel panic.

The *zapilotes* sensed death in the immobile body. Their soaring circles began to lower.

Slocum heaved a deep breath. He felt a miraculous sense of relief—at least he could breathe! Then he suddenly recalled the little round leaves. Robles was not a kind man. The leaves had to be some kind of a narcotic plant. Evidently one of its effects was to induce partial paralysis. Slocum did not know that *yaa-askidi*—a Yaqui word—was given that name after it had moved north from Aztec territory, because it referred to one of the masked gods of the tribe. People who took the drug became as a god while they were under its influence.

Slocum could move his eyes. He moved them sideways. No one was in sight. Obviously Robles knew that no guards were necessary for anyone who had just taken *yaa-askidi*.

The *zapilotes* had descended even lower. When Slocum happened to be sleeping in the desert in the daytime the *zapilotes* would come near. A simple flick of his fingers would send them flapping away.

He tried to yell. No sound emerged; his face remained fixed, as if it were sculpted from clay.

The shadow of a gliding *zapilote* passed across his face. Then another shadow, this time closer. Five minutes passed. One of the huge, ugly birds glided overhead so close that Slocum felt the wind from the eight-foot wing spread.

The bird landed a few feet past him in the usual clumsy manner of *zapilotes*—tottering on its legs and almost stumbling like a baby learning how to walk. It pivoted and began to hop toward him. It was encouraged by the complete lack of movement in its prey.

With his peripheral vision Slocum saw Robles arriving to enjoy the sight. But when the *zapilote* saw him walking toward Slocum, the frightened bird hopped away frantically. The other *zapilotes* let themselves soar upward on the heated thermals which radiated from the rocky flat. The *zapilote* that had landed near Slocum hopped behind one of the large gray boulders that lay scattered everywhere.

Robles called out, "What a pity! They will not have their lunch if I am around to watch. I will come visit again, say in an hour. If that is acceptable to you? By then the *zapilotes* will have eaten a bit. Then we shall talk. *Hasta la vista.*"

Half an hour passed. The sun began to sink from its zenith. The rocky surface absorbed the heat and radiated it along its surface until Slocum's back was burning. More blisters began to form in the stubble of his beard and on his thighs.

The *zapilotes* had recovered from their wariness at Robles's approach. Nothing was moving in the area.

They began their approach once more. Some were on the ground. They held their wings half-stretched for ventilation as they hopped closer. Others still circled effortlessly overhead, gradually spiralling downward. A large bird was the first to touch Slocum. It landed in its awkward fashion only four feet from the inert, sun-blistered, naked man. It hopped closer, attracted by the bloody gash on Slocum's cheek.

Slocum saw the cruel hooked beak approach. The red neck stretched. He could smell the *zapilote's* stinking breath, foul because its usual food was rotting carrion. Slocum willed himself with all his strength to move. He could not. He prayed silently, *Please, God, not my eyes. Zapilotes* liked to begin with the eyes.

But because Robles had cut Slocum's cheek with his gun barrel, the *zapilote* went for the bloody gash instead. The biggest *zapilote* suddenly landed beside Slocum. There was always a dominant male in bird societies, and so the first bird's beak had only sheared off a small piece of Slocum's cheek instead of the much larger chunk it would have ordinarily sliced off.

The pain was vicious. The two birds fought over the small bit of flesh with their wings. The smaller one was brutally shoved away and, while it squawked angrily, it dropped the bloody bit onto Slocum's left wrist. There it fell between two turns of the rawhide thong.

Robles watched from the veranda. It suddenly occurred to him that a man soon to be blinded could not very well guide him to the secret place where the rest of Maximilian's treasure must be hidden. He said, "Henrique!"

"*Sí.*"

"Stay near the *gringo*. Keep the *zapilotes* away."

"*Sí.*"

"When it gets dark, come back." *Zapilotes* disappeared at dusk. "He and I will talk in the morning. This *yaa-askidi*—how long does it last?"

Henrique shrugged. "Twenty-four hours, maybe," he said. "The *bruja* said—"

Robles held up his hand. He thought. Like most Mexicans, he did not care much for precision, nor did the *bruja*. The *yaa-askidi* worked for a while, it was more than a few hours; twenty-four was a good round number. *Nombre de Dios*, what difference did it make, anyway?

Robles mused. Twenty-four hours. That meant the *gringo* would be totally paralyzed until the next afternoon.

There was no way he could work free of the rawhide, to start with. They had dug in so far into his ankles and wrists that the circulation would be impaired. When they would cut the thongs the next day he'd have to be carried. And when to that problem he added the twenty-four hours' total paralysis—*bien!* He stood up, called to the men, and told them all to get a good night's sleep.

"We will be riding tomorrow with the *gringo*," he added. "We will take picks and shovels. Henrique, get them ready."

Armendariz looked at him.

"What's the matter?" Robles demanded in an annoyed tone.

"This one will not talk."

"How the hell do you know?"

"I saw his eyes."

"His eyes, yes! When he sees the *zapilotes* coming at his eyes, he will change his mind fast enough. Believe me. He will change his mind fast. We must make sure to chase them away just before they go for his eyes, you understand? He will be thinking about them all night. He will talk as soon as they show up overhead tomorrow morning. And if he still won't talk, we will put him on the greased stake."

Armendariz shrugged. He had seen a lot of hard men in his time: some *rurales* officers, some Yaquis. They had died well. But this quiet *gringo*—something in the man's eyes told Armendariz that Robles would be proven wrong. But one did not argue with Robles.

"So you agree, Jorge?"

"Se puede que sí, se puede que no. Maybe yes, maybe no."

"You want to make a bet, Jorge?"

"If you wish. I have no money."

But he valued his knife, Robles knew. A knife maker had etched that cruel statement on it in Mexico City, to order. It had cost fifty pesos extra. So Robles said, "My Colt against your knife?"

Armendariz had no handgun. He greatly admired his leader's .45.

"Bien."

Robles knew what he would do. As soon as the *gringo* broke down, he would turn to Armendariz and hold out his hand. As soon as the knife would be placed in his palm, he would hand it back and give Armendariz the *abrazo*. Jorge would like that, and it would keep him loyal.

Yes, Robles thought with a satisfied smile, *a very good idea.*

Slocum's teeth began to chatter from the cold. He still did not know that the effects of the drug would soon wear off.

A dark shape emerged from the trees that bordered the edge of the flat. It began to move toward him cautiously. Slocum's peripheral vision caught it. He could not make out what it was. It was low and close to the ground. He considered that it might be a *tigre*, or even one of the occasional grizzlies that roamed the Sierra.

With an inward sigh of relief he saw that it was a coyote when it moved toward his feet. Then he remembered that coyotes ate dead animals, and that this one might consider that Slocum's lack of movement made him rank as carrion.

The coyote circled around toward Slocum's left wrist. It had just smelled the blood and the bit of Slocum's flesh that had been dropped there by the quarrelling *zapilotes*.

It stretched out its neck and licked the blood-soaked rawhide. Then it realized that there was a piece of raw meat nestling deep within the many turns of the rawhide. It was hard to reach, but the coyote's sharp teeth solved that problem.

In less than a minute it had sliced through the several turns. Then it nuzzled Slocum's wrist, searching for more blood. Before Slocum realized what he was doing, he had pushed the coyote's muzzle away.

The coyote leaped backward in astonishment. At that moment, Slocum realized with joy that he had begun to regain control of his body. He willed himself to lift his arm. It obeyed. When it came down he felt a small stone underneath his forearm. He picked it up and threw it. It thumped the animal in the ribs. The astonished coyote promptly turned and slunk away.

Slocum was exultant. He could turn his head now. He kept opening and closing his free hand until the blood began to flow freely through the arteries. When he had good control over his hand, he reached across his chest and began to pick at the thong around his left wrist. The water-shrunken rawhide was difficult to undo. It cost him two fingernails, torn away from the fingers underneath, and two hours of valuable time.

One more hour and he had freed his ankles. He spent twenty minutes massaging his legs to encourage the circulation to return. As it slowly returned it felt as if tiny knives were being inserted into his legs. Then he stood up. He staggered and stumbled, then fell. His blood-starved legs were not yet able to support his weight. He sat down and massaged them strenuously for another ten minutes. That did the job. When he stood up again, he not only could stand, he could walk, although the latter took much effort and there was a lot of stumbling at first.

Now he needed three things: food, water, and a weapon. Clothes were not important.

Grass was rare in the area. Therefore, Robles had to have oats for his horses. Near the corral there was a small waterproof shed. Oats in sacks were stored there, as well as the usual litter of old bridles, reatas, tattered saddle blankets, horseshoes and horseshoe nails. Rusted picks and shovels were strewn around haphazardly. None of them would do for a weapon.

There were no sentries anywhere. They were not essential, as Robles had long ago decided. Since the only way to approach his hideout was along the old, narrow trails, he felt sure that any approach, open or surreptitious, would be noticed far away, and reluctant *campesinos* like Oswaldo would quickly enough give warning. And he was right.

Slocum reached into a sack and pulled out a double handful of the oats. He chewed them, letting the nourishment flow into his stomach. In a few minutes he felt much stronger. He took another double handful and chewed them slowly while he planned his next step.

First, a weapon. That was easy enough. When he had chewed his third double handful he felt strong enough to loosen the soil packed around the sharpened stake. His back and shoulder muscles ached badly, but he had expected that. He was pleased to note that he had enough strength to pull out the stake.

Now he had an effective spear.

Water next. And a good hiding place while he gained strength.

The cover would have to be perfect, because they would come looking for him. They were fine trackers and knew the country well. Anything out of the ordinary would be noticed immediately.

And after water, and after cover where he regained his strength, the next item on the agenda was the death of Robles. This would be impossible to achieve with all his men surrounding him. The only thing to do was to draw the men away. Then all Slocum would have to do was slide in between them. Slocum laughed silently while he thought over the implications of the phrase "all he would have to do."

The solution would be to do just what he was doing: get the hell out of there, and then circle back to Robles while the men were out searching for him.

No doubt they would expect him to head for San Felipe. Therefore, he would head in the opposite direction. Then it would be best to follow the basic law of military strategy: *hold the high ground*.

In his particular case, without any weapon except a spear, it meant that he should always be above any trail or road, and that he should travel higher than any such trail.

Most people when trailing tended to look straight ahead or somewhat down. And if anyone should look up and see him, and if he was close enough, Slocum would use his added elevation to give added impetus and weight to his downhill charge with his improvised spear. It might give him a small advantage—but still, it wouldn't be much against a man armed with a carbine.

"You tied him up!" Robles shouted. "You, Henrique! Not me! And he got away!"

"I do not understand this. I put water on the leather—"

Robles smashed his fist on the table as hard as he could.

"Shut up, *cabrón!*" he yelled. "You will find him, you will bring him back! Do you understand why?" He turned to Armendariz. "That potion was supposed to keep him paralyzed all night. I hold *you* even more responsible, Jorge."

Armendariz had once made a mistake with Robles which he now deeply regretted. He had mentioned proudly that his sister and brother-in-law owned a small *ranchito* thirty miles west of San Felipe, near Agua Zarca. He had been flattered by Robles's interest in the name of the *ranchito*—Las Miraflores—and whether they had any children. Yes, Armendariz had replied with enthusiasm, yes, they had a boy and a girl, and the boy was named after him.

Now Robles said slowly, "You will find this *gringo*.

I want him alive. Or I shall visit Las Miraflores. Do you understand me thoroughly? I should be sorry if you did not."

Armendariz said nothing.

Robles said harshly, *"Do* you understand? Yes or no?"

Armendariz said slowly, *"Sí."*

Robles flicked his hand as if he were brushing away a fly.

Armendariz turned and went out. He was sick with apprehension over what Robles would do to Las Miraflores if he failed. And so he hated Slocum for putting him into that position.

14

Slocum's blistered feet propelled him higher up a mountain. He climbed it at an angle to make it easier. He pulled at bushes with his free hand to help take the weight off his bleeding feet. He came to a place where the mountain flattened out into a tiny valley. A trickle of water had dug itself a narrow channel there over the centuries. It was lined with reeds, and where it came close to a vertical rock face it was bordered with a dense growth of ferns. Little green frogs jumped into the water when Slocum neared.

Slocum's tongue had swollen so much that it filled his entire mouth. He had crossed deserts before, and he knew what to do. He kneeled down, cupped some water in his palm, and licked it. Swallowing would be too dangerous; he would lose control and suffer violent cramps. Next, he cupped water in both palms and let his tongue rest in it. He did this several times until it had resumed its normal size. Next, he permitted himself to drink a sip at a time. Satisfied at last, he poured water over his head, back, and shoulders. He felt much better. He soaked his feet in the cool water. He felt his cheek gingerly. It was swollen and tender. He had better get to a doctor as soon as he could.

He stood up. The first thing he noticed was the kneeling figure of Armendariz. The man was half a mile away, and was scrutinizing Slocum's tracks. Slocum was barefoot. All Armendariz had to do was follow tracks made by a man without shoes, since everyone else in that country wore either boots or *huaraches*.

Armendariz stood up. His eyes searched the mountain. Slocum froze. Movement was what frequently attracted attention; a man not moving was frequently not noticed. Armendariz's head was swinging back and forth. He did not see Slocum. Then he looked down at the tracks once more.

Slocum knew that his tanned face and arms and his white body made an unusual pattern against the gray rocks and occasional pines and oaks. He needed camouflage. And he suddenly realized that it was available right at his feet.

The little creek had eroded itself a channel. And the channel was cut through clay. It matched perfectly the dominant color of the stone which formed the mountains of the Sierra.

Slocum reached down, and easily broke off a chunk

of the clay. It crumbled and dissolved immediately into a thick mud as soon as he put it in the water. Working quickly, he smeared his entire body with it. He smeared it liberally over his hair and face. Then he rubbed it over his crude spear.

Next, he stood in the sun. It was strong enough to bake the clay onto him in five minutes. He bent down and looked at himself in the water. A strange gray monster peered back at him. Slocum permitted himself a smile; a row of white teeth appeared in the gray mass. It was perfect except for his eyelids. He smeared a thin paste over them. He narrowed his eyes to slits and looked again at his improvised mirror. Perfect.

It was an old Apache trick. They used it to approach army posts in the daytime. They could get within fifty feet of one, and then lance an unsuspecting soldier as he walked by on his way to the corral.

Satisfied, Slocum looked again at his remorseless tracker. Armendariz was coming on doggedly at a half crouch. He was carrying a carbine at the ready. It looked very much like Slocum's own carbine; there was a rippling pattern on the right side of the walnut stock that was unique.

The oats and the water had strengthened Slocum. He did not want to kill the man. The torture had weakened Slocum, and he needed to conserve his strength for the decisive attempt against Robles.

This would be a good time to test his camouflage before he put it to practice in his final approach to Robles's headquarters.

A series of flat rocks led to an oak whose branches shot out at right angles over the creek. He walked on the rocks till he reached the lowest branch. He took his spear and sent it spiralling into the *mesquital* on the upland side of the oaks. Then he reached up, caught the branch, and, swinging himself up on it with a muttered curse at the agony it caused to his back and shoulders, he crawled along it to the trunk, slid around it, and continued on another branch until he dropped off the tree sixty feet from his starting point.

That should cause some delay. Armendariz would think that his quarry had stepped into the stream and was wading along it till he could find a good place to emerge from. So, Slocum reasoned, he would follow the stream searching for tracks.

After a while Armendariz, if he were a good tracker, would realize he had better go back to where he had lost the tracks, and start once more. This second time he would probably cut his trail by walking in a circle.

Slocum lay flat on the gray rock ten feet from the trail. He watched Armendariz as the man kept moving intently at his half-crouch. Every few seconds he lifted his head and scanned the countryside. He was inspecting sites that would afford good hiding places for an ambush.

That was one reason why Slocum had picked an open flat. Since no ambush could be mounted from such an area, he counted upon Armendariz spending little time in scanning it.

Slocum watched the man moving toward his hiding place. Armendariz's head was swinging back and forth like a grizzly's as he sensed the nearness of his quarry. When he was fifty feet away, Slocum narrowed his green eyes to slits. The clay that had caked itself on his eyelashes would be effective, he felt.

Thirty feet. The sun had baked the clay dry. The heat felt wonderfully soothing to his wrenched back and shoulders. Slocum took a long breath and held it. This would be the acid test for his camouflage.

Twenty feet. The man was a killer. There was no wasted motion in anything he had done so far. He looked ahead, then to the left, then to the right, then up. Every so often he stopped and scrutinized his back trail. Hunted men, as Armendariz knew, were like animals. They would make their trail. Knowing they were being followed, they would circle back, take a position beside their trail, and then suddenly charge from ambush at an unsuspecting pursuer as he moved intent on their footprints.

Ten feet. Armendariz scanned the gray, rocky mountainside. Slocum tightened the grip on his spear shaft. If Armendariz were suddenly to realize that a man lay there under the clay, Slocum would have three seconds to get to his feet and lunge at him. But all that Armendariz had to do was to swing the muzzle of the Winchester and pull the trigger. That would take half a second. The odds were bad. And it would be terrible, Slocum thought wryly, to be killed by his own gun.

Armendariz looked directly at Slocum. Then his gaze moved on. For a few seconds Slocum could not believe it. He thought that the man was playing a cat-and-mouse game, and would let Slocum believe that the camouflage had been successful. And then he would suddenly spin around and fire just as Slocum was congratulating himself.

Slocum forced himself to keep his eyes slitted. He forced himself—and this was far more difficult—not to turn his head to follow Armendariz's movements. If Armendariz were to turn for his usual scan of the back trail, he would realize that the outline of the gray rock had changed shape. He would be curious enough to come back and investigate.

Slocum was right. Armendariz did turn around. He had sensed something out of the ordinary about that area. He had passed it many times, and there was no rock there. But he could not put his finger on what had troubled him. So he shrugged and continued tracking.

Higher up, just beyond the crest, Oswaldo had seen everything: Slocum drinking; Slocum rubbing himself with the clay; Slocum crawling along the branches of the oak; Slocum waiting beside the trail for Armendariz.

Oswaldo had recognized him immediately as the prisoner who had spent the night outside his house being tortured.

Oswaldo sighed. He lifted his old rifle and put Slocum's right thigh in the V notch. He was a fine shot; he had trained himself by taking only one cartridge whenever he went out to hunt. The knowledge that he had only one chance made him fire only when he was absolutely sure of his target.

He had gone out that morning to hunt deer.

If he shot the *gringo* Robles would be grateful. As much as Robles could be grateful, that is. It might turn out to be profitable. Clearly, this *gringo* meant a great deal to Robles.

But there were two problems.

First, the rifle. It was a fifteen-year-old U. S. Army Springfield. Six years before, Oswaldo had traded two fine mules for it from a *gringo* prospector who was tired of searching for gold. But Robles wanted rifles all the time. Robles did not know about this fine rifle.

Oswaldo kept it wrapped in oiled silk, and he hid it in a clump of cactus a hundred feet from his hut. He fired it only when he was sure no one could hear it. And always a few miles at least from the Robles camp.

If he shot Slocum Robles would want to know all about the rifle. Then he would demand it. There was no question about this in Oswaldo's mind.

Second, one of Robles's men had taken Oswaldo's treasured kerosene lamp with him when they left with Slocum. Oswaldo's wife loved that lamp after years of trying to sew by candlelight. The man who stole it was Armendariz. When Oswaldo politely suggested that the man had probably taken it absentmindedly, Armendariz had laughed.

Oswaldo then mentioned the affair to Robles as he was climbing into his saddle. Robles said curtly, "Do not bother me with this childish complaint, you fool!"

So Oswaldo let the hammer down gently on the unexploded cartridge. He would profit far more if he used it to bring home venison.

Let Robles pay for the lamp and for that remark. He put the rifle down. He put one palm on top of the other and his chin on the back of his right hand, and then watched for the *gringo* to make his next move.

Slocum stood up. Oswaldo marvelled at the superb camouflage. He did not know that Slocum had learned this trick from Apaches. The *gringo* then moved at a half-crouch. Oswaldo understood: he was ready to go flat instantaneously and blend with the rocky soil. He was heading toward Robles's headquarters. Oswaldo knew what that meant. The *gringo* wanted revenge.

"Vaya con Dios," he muttered. He pivoted and watched Armendariz. The tracker had stopped at the edge of a clay deposit where Slocum had applied his camouflage. He squatted and ran his fingers lightly over the clay. He felt the striations left by Slocum's fingernails. Armendariz stood up and thought. He looked at the water. It was obvious to him that the gringo had dug out some clay and used it.

Armendariz stood there and puzzled it out for a while. Then it came to him in a flash: *camouflage!* He immediately moved in a wide circle. He cut Slocum's tracks on the far side of the oak tree. He spun around and trotted through the *mesquital*. He found Slocum's position, where the man had lain flat beside the trail.

Ten feet! And he had looked straight at the *gringo* and not seen him!

Armendariz stood and cursed. The *gringo* had made a fool of him. When he caught up with him again, he would not kill him—Robles's orders had been careful on that point—but he would shoot both of the man's kneecaps. That would ensure that the *gringo* would wait till a horse would come and carry him back. It would also ensure that the *gringo* would think of Armendariz every time he picked up his crutches for the rest of his life. If Robles decided to let him live.

Oswaldo watched. He saw Armendariz cut trail. He watched him spin around and start to follow the *gringo*.

Oswaldo estimated that Armendariz would catch up with Slocum in about ten minutes.

Oswaldo stood up. He watched the *gringo's* painful advance. There was no fit place for an ambush, even if Slocum were aware that Armendariz had turned around and was trotting now behind him, ready to break his kneecaps as the first order of business. And any lump of gray stone was going to get a careful going-over. If the hunter knew that every low, rounded lump of stone could be a man, the surprise element was finished.

No, Oswaldo decided. The *gringo* was out of luck this time. He removed the cartridge from the firing chamber. With his knife he scored a deep cross on the lead. It would open up like the petals of a flower on impact. He inserted the bullet into the Springfield.

He aimed downhill at Armendariz. He allowed for the bullet's drop. He allowed next for a slight crosswind that had just sprung up. He led a little bit. He squeezed the trigger gently.

Armendariz trotted right into the heavy slug. It entered the right side of his head just forward of the ear. When it came out, it took the entire right side of his head with it.

Oswaldo put the empty shell in his pocket. He saved money by loading his old cartridges. He walked down the mountainside. When he looked down at the man, he noticed that the legs were twitching. There was life in the nervous system and possibly in what was left of the brain. He drew back his right leg and kicked Armendariz in the balls as hard as he could.

Then he picked up the carbine. He used Armendariz's sweat-soaked shirt to wipe off the gray brain matter splattered over it. He felt rather pleased at the way the day was ending.

Slocum heard the rifle shot. It sounded far enough to his rear not to worry him. Someone out hunting?

He hobbled on painfully on his bare feet.

When he finally neared the mine headquarters he dropped flat to reconnoiter. There were no signs of life. The corral was empty of all horses except Robles's fine chestnut stallion.

If Robles were a good general, he would be sitting

inside waiting for reports to come in. He would not be out himself in the field. Good. He was inside the house. Slocum permitted himself a small smile of satisfaction. It hurt his badly infected cheek.

Next, he had to crawl all the way across the open flat on the gray rock. He had to be ready to freeze into immobility in case someone might come riding in.

The rock waste from the mine had first been dumped close to the shaft. Successive waves of rock were dumped farther and farther away. The mine had been in operation for over two hundred years. So Slocum had to crawl over five hundred feet before he reached the bungalow where Robles was waiting.

He crawled fifty feet before he heard a horse's hooves clattering on the rock.

He froze. The horse came up behind him, cut across his vision in front, and stopped in front of the mine headquarters. The rider hitched his horse to the rack, dismounted, and knocked.

"*Quien es?*" It was Robles's voice. Slocum grinned in excitement.

"*Soy yo, Tomás!*"

"*Pase.*"

Tomás entered. Slocum could not hear what they were saying, but Robles was clearly furious. Then the door slammed, and a red-faced Tomás emerged. He mounted and rode back furiously, passing within twenty feet of Slocum. The horse shied, but Tomás lashed him with a vicious cut of his quirt and rode on.

Slocum crawled. He had gone another seventy-five feet when he heard another horse to his left. He turned his head cautiously to look at it. Then he understood why the previous horse had been nervous: he had scraped his knees raw on the rock and he had left a bloody trail behind him.

The second rider angled closer to Slocum than the first. It was Lucas Carrizo. The horse shied at the blood, as the first horse had done. But horses were always doing that for lizards or snakes. When Carrizo saw neither, he paid no further attention.

Robles heard Carrizo approaching. He stepped out on the veranda and leaned on the railing. He wore a Colt. Carrizo wore one as well. They talked for a while. Then Robles walked back inside and emerged with one of Slocum's fake red glass necklaces.

He held it up. Even at the distance Slocum was, he could see Carrizo's stance of astonishment. Then Robles handed it to Carrizo, who put it carefully inside his shirt. Clearly, his duty was to sell it on behalf of Robles.

Slocum did not envy Carrizo's disappointment, which would be taking place in two days or so in an expensive jeweler's in Mexico City.

Carrizo mounted and rode away. Robles watched him with a grin. He was anticipating the fortune that would be his when Carrizo returned. Then he went back inside.

Slocum moved closer. This time he got within forty feet before he had to freeze. Robles had stepped out. He took a leak from the veranda, staring toward the direction where Slocum had escaped. Then he went inside again.

Slocum crawled. He reached the bottom step. No one was in sight.

He stood up. Blood was trickling down from his knees. They had been scraped raw. The clay armor had begun to crack in many places. Overall he resembled some kind of a primeval gray monster that had risen from the mud of an ancient ocean floor. Slocum had no idea what he looked like. All he felt was hatred. His green eyes glared.

He had been waiting for this moment for months.

He brought up his spear and held it with both hands. He climbed the veranda steps silently. He walked across. He kicked open the door with his left foot and walked in.

Robles was sitting in a wooden chair across the room. His back was to the wall, which was made of slabs of crudely cut pine. He was lifting a glass of beer to his lips.

Slocum took two long steps and lunged at Robles with all the strength he could summon. This would be his only chance.

If Robles had simply seen Slocum burst in fully clad he would have dropped the glass of beer and fired immediately. But the apparition was so far from anything that he had ever experienced that he hesitated for a second.

That delay was all that Slocum needed. The spear entered Robles's body just below the arch of his rib cage. It penetrated his solar plexus and so short-circuited all his nervous control. The sharp point went through his stomach, and finally severed his spinal cord.

Then it penetrated the pine wall and came to rest.

Robles's bowels emptied. He would live for another five minutes, unable to move or to talk.

Slocum found his clothes in a corner. He put them on. He pulled on his boots, wincing as they slid over his blistered and cut feet. He could wash the clay off later in a safe place.

He walked over to the man, unbuckled the gunbelt, and put it on, heedless of the hatred that glittered in Robles's black eyes.

His saddlebags stood in a corner. The gold coins were still in the bottom. He took out all the necklaces and hung them around Robles's neck. He emptied the loose jewels into his lap. The hatred in Robles's eyes vanished, to be replaced by a puzzled look.

Slocum stepped back. Robles's men would fight over them when they realized that Robles was dead, pinned to the wall like a dead insect. Slocum would like to see that, but he had been in Mexico long enough.

One more thing to do before he went home.

He leaned forward and said, "Wesley Putnam, you son of a bitch."

Comprehension bloomed at last in Robles's eyes. He opened his mouth to spit in Slocum's face, but he died.

Slocum slung the saddlebags over his shoulder. He hurt like hell all over. Time to go to Arizona.

JAKE LOGAN

___	0-867-21087	SLOCUM'S REVENGE	$1.95
___	07296-3	THE JACKSON HOLE TROUBLE	$2.50
___	07182-0	SLOCUM AND THE CATTLE QUEEN	$2.75
___	06413-1	SLOCUM GETS EVEN	$2.50
___	06744-0	SLOCUM AND THE LOST DUTCHMAN MINE	$2.50
___	07018-2	BANDIT GOLD	$2.50
___	06846-3	GUNS OF THE SOUTH PASS	$2.50
___	07258-4	DALLAS MADAM	$2.50
___	07139-1	SOUTH OF THE BORDER	$2.50
___	07460-9	SLOCUM'S CRIME	$2.50
___	07567-2	SLOCUM'S PRIDE	$2.50
___	07382-3	SLOCUM AND THE GUN-RUNNERS	$2.50
___	07494-3	SLOCUM'S WINNING HAND	$2.50
___	08382-9	SLOCUM IN DEADWOOD	$2.50
___	07753-5	THE JOURNEY OF DEATH	$2.50
___	07683-0	GUNPLAY AT HOBB'S HOLE	$2.50
___	07654-7	SLOCUM'S STAMPEDE	$2.50
___	07784-5	SLOCUM'S GOOD DEED	$2.50
___	08101-X	THE NEVADA SWINDLE	$2.50
___	07973-2	SLOCUM AND THE AVENGING GUN	$2.50
___	08031-5	SLOCUM RIDES ALONE	$2.50

Prices may be slightly higher in Canada.

Available at your local bookstore or return this form to:

BERKLEY
Book Mailing Service
P.O. Box 690, Rockville Centre, NY 11571

Please send me the titles checked above. I enclose _____. Include 75¢ for postage and handling if one book is ordered; 25¢ per book for two or more not to exceed $1.75. California, Illinois, New York and Tennessee residents please add sales tax.

NAME_____

ADDRESS_____

CITY_____STATE/ZIP_____

(allow six weeks for delivery)

GREAT WESTERN YARNS FROM ONE OF THE BEST-SELLING WRITERS IN THE FIELD TODAY

JAKE LOGAN

___ 06551-0	**LAW COMES TO COLD RAIN**	$2.25
___ 0-867-21003	**BLOODY TRAIL TO TEXAS**	$1.95
___ 0-867-21041	**THE COMANCHE'S WOMAN**	$1.95
___ 0-872-16979	**OUTLAW BLOOD**	$1.95
___ 06191-4	**THE CANYON BUNCH**	$2.25
___ 05956-1	**SHOTGUNS FROM HELL**	$2.25
___ 06132-9	**SILVER CITY SHOOTOUT**	$2.25
___ 07398-X	**SLOCUM AND THE LAW**	$2.50
___ 06255-4	**SLOCUM'S JUSTICE**	$2.25
___ 05958-8	**SLOCUM'S RAID**	$1.95
___ 06481-6	**SWAMP FOXES**	$2.25
___ 0-872-16823	**SLOCUM'S CODE**	$1.95
___ 06532-4	**SLOCUM'S COMMAND**	$2.25
___ 0-867-21071	**SLOCUM'S DEBT**	$1.95
___ 0-425-05998-7	**SLOCUM'S DRIVE**	$2.25
___ 0-867-21090	**SLOCUM'S GOLD**	$1.95
___ 0-867-21023	**SLOCUM'S HELL**	$1.95